WASHED UP WITH A BROKEN HEART IN ROCK HALL

BY

PETER SVENSON

THE PERMANENT PRESS
SAG HARBOR, NEW YORK 11963

Copyright© 2004 by Peter Svenson

Library of Congress Cataloging-in-Publication Data

Svenson, Peter.
   Washed up with a broken heart in Rock Hall : a novel / by
Peter Svenson.
      p. cm.
   ISBN 1-57962-108-2 (alk. paper)
   1. Chesapeake Bay Region (Md. and Va.)—Fiction. 2. Rock
Hall (Kent County, Md.)—Fiction. 3. Man-woman
relationships—Fiction. 4. Fiction—Authorship—Fiction. 5.
Loss (Psychology)—Fiction. 6. Middle aged men—Fiction. 7.
Midlife crisis—Fiction. 8. Divorced men—Fiction. I. Title.

   PS3619.V46W38 2004
   813'.6—dc22

                                        2003066877

Printed in The United States of America

THE PERMANENT PRESS
4170 Noyac Road
Sag Harbor, NY 11963

For Anne

The characters in this book are wholly fictional and bear no resemblance, real or imagined, to actual people. Needless to say, the central character bears absolutely no resemblance to me.

The stting, however, is real. I hope that my depiction -- with its accuracies or inaccuracies -- will not give offense to the local denizens.

WASHED UP WITH A BROKEN HEART IN ROCK HALL

Chapter 1

A sunset sail at sunrise is something to remember a boat by. Budge Moss, author and weekend sailor, newly divested of wife, home, and personal effects save what he's got aboard, has set his course due east across Chesapeake Bay with a cat for company.

He is heading for Rock Hall on Maryland's eastern shore, where a buyer awaits the boat and a new chapter awaits him. As he wrote in his journal the previous night,

No, this is not the lowest point in my life, although it would seem so. This is a beginning, a new beginning — and I don't mean to sound like a politician. The ending is over. I have already bottomed out. Three months ago when my beloved wife quit our marriage, setting the events in motion that will culminate in my stepping aboard Hula Moon *early tomorrow morning, I had no idea what was in store for me or where I would go. Now, at least, I know where I'm going — that is, if I can steer a straight course.*

An evocative name for a sailboat, *Hula Moon* — referring to a honeymoon in Hawaii a long, long time ago. At the helm, Budge does his best to forget all that. Now it's just a well-depreciated fiberglass possession that has outlived its usefulness and is — thank God! — sold. The ad read, "27' Catalina, engine rebuilt, GPS, UHF, VHF, DF, stereo, furling jib, dinghy, make offer." An offer was made and Budge didn't dicker. Old boats are like old people — only angels want them.

Do I have misgivings? Hell no. Hula Moon *sat dock-side most of the time, and anyway, what's in working order today is not necessarily in working order tomorrow. Do I have misgivings about losing my wife? Hell yes. She sat centermost in my life, and her love seemed in perfect working order until the day I realized otherwise. Fixing it was out of the question, she said, and she immediately hired a lawyer to prove her point. One day we're happily (so I thought) married, the next day she wants out.*

Now my destination is Rock Hall, a bayside town seventy miles by land and ten miles by water. I know next to nothing about the place, but I imagine it is home to sailors, cheaters, watermen, wife-beaters, time-sharers, lotus eaters, fishermen, and mistake repeaters. I'll be just one of many middle-aged souls there who've committed no crime except to forget the inevitability of change. Name: Budge R.S.G.N. (Rolling Stone Gathers No) Moss. Age: old enough to know better. Status: dumpee.

For the record, Budge is 55 years old. He is hale and sound-minded, generally an optimist, although he has gotten in the habit lately of feeling sorry for himself. The boat is the one major possession he was allowed to keep; the rest he either gave up voluntarily or had taken from him legally.

Now he is about to give up the boat — the agreed-upon recompense is $5,575, and on this, he intends to live until his life gets straightened out. This translates, more or less, into the publication of his next book, the book he began writing yesterday. What will he be writing about? A middle-aged husband abruptly rendered single and not by choice. A loving man who doesn't deserve the fate he got dished. Budge keeps the journal to feed thoughts directly into the project. Here are some sentences he jots down even as he's at the helm, tacking *Hula Moon* across the northwesterly breezes of the bay.

Ah, the blue-brown Chesapeake! A two-foot swell randomly gilded with whitecaps. Mostly clear and sunny, with a long yellow tint of nitrous oxide drifting along the western shore's horizon. Baltimore, Dundalk, Sparrows Point, Curtis Bay — beautifully plumed offenders, yet the worst pollution, I'm told, is ground runoff from almost every vantage of the watershed. The broad bay absorbs more and more crap, and I float upon it disingenuously, demanding my right to water recreation. There are others out here today — trawlers, sailing sloops, cabin cruisers, cigarette racers — plus the workboats and a smattering of shipping traffic: tug and barge combinations, car carriers, container ships.

I steer my valedictory course, mindful of all these plus the birds overhead. I've enjoyed old Hula Moon, *but the next phase will be boatless, by choice as well as necessity. What I'd really like to do is find a little place to rent right on the water. A cottage on the Chesapeake, where I can pull myself together, get some writing done, and watch sunsets.*

Over the traumatic months, he researched the Internet and came upon Rock Hall's municipal website quite by accident (yes, he got to keep his laptop computer — he couldn't make a living without it). Comparing the town with others on the eastern shore, he made up his mind, sight unseen, that it was as good a place as any to start over. Beyond that, his plans haven't been more specific. Verily, he's embarked on the Thoreauvian simplification he has dreamed about for decades. It took personal upheaval to get him to, well, budge. With pregnant sails, taut lines, and spray intermittently flung in his face, he has no regrets — or so he tells himself.

After four hours of sailing, though, he's glad to be approaching the harbor at Rock Hall. Fatigue is setting in, and he's wet and windburned. The town's pale blue watertower, the landmark he has been cognizant of for the past two hours, looms tall and welcoming. Perking up with a thermos of coffee, he makes note of the buoys; yes, he has steered a true course, followed chart and compass perfectly. As he enters the channel between the breakwater, he experiences a pleasant sense of accomplishment. For a final voyage, this has been the best and luckiest. Characteristically, he's quitting while he's ahead.

He drops the sail, motoring the last several hundred yards to the rightmost dock, as prearranged, where a man stands expectantly. Budge glances at his watch; it's 10:30 a.m. His timing couldn't be better.

The buyer, a rangy open-shirted fellow, helps dockside with the mooring lines, then comes aboard, beaming approvingly.

"Nice boat, just as you described it."

"I think you'll like it."

"I do already. I even like the name. I might keep it, if you don't mind."

"Suit yourself," Budge replies.

"I see you've got a lot of stuff aboard. You moving someplace?"

"Here. Temporarily."

Budge adds the "temporarily" only because he thinks it sounds better, although "here," by itself, would have been the more truthful answer.

"Nice little town. Nice people live here."

"So I've been told."

"That's the town's official motto. 'Nice People Live Here.'"

"Sounds like a good one."

"You familiar with this neck of the woods?"

"Not really," Budge admits.

"Well, just remember one thing. You gotta be born here to have the best credentials. Otherwise, you're an outsider. You could live here fifty years, and you'd still be an outsider."

"Okay, I'll remember that."

The buyer descends belowdeck, where there is really only room for him alone. "Yep, it looks like you're moving lock, stock, and barrel," he observes.

Through the hatch, Budge agrees, offering no further explanation. The buyer clambers topside, satisfied with his inspection. His body language implies that the boat now belongs to him.

"I've got the cashier's check if you've got the title," he says.

"It's right here in my pocket," replies Budge.

The swap happens so fast that Budge has no time to reflect. He doesn't reminisce about the good times he and his wife spent aboard, or the bad times they spent arguing. She didn't like taking orders from him, yet sometimes he couldn't help himself. Now it's all ancient history.

"Give me ten minutes to collect my stuff," he says.

"Let me give you a hand. Whatcha got here... oh, a cat. A sailboat cat, hey, that's cool!"

A pile of belongings on the dock. It smacks of eviction, which it is. With a little help, I'm evicting myself. Clothing on hangers, including my one serviceable suit. Two trash bags bulging with bedding and underwear. A suitcase of shoes. A laundry basket full of dirty laundry. The old stereo set and its speakers. A reading lamp, my desk chair, phone/fax (and umbilical tangle), laptop and printer,

toaster oven, microwave, old framed photographs, guitar.
Four or five boxes — utensils, small appliances, bric-à-
brac, books, manuscripts. And securely on top, Ragu in
her carrier, mewing nervously.

Budge's first task, after making sure his pet is supplied
with food and water, and covering everything with a tarp,
is to get directions to the nearest bank. He'll deposit the
check, draw some cash, and open both a savings and
checking account. Conveniently, the Rock Hall trolley
makes a stop at Peoples Bank on Route 20.

I'm liking this place already! From the trolley, I get a
good idea of the town's layout (the driver's spiel is helpful
in this regard). At the bank they treat me as a valued cus-
tomer, and afterwards, flush with new funds and tempo-
rary checks, I walk to the Rock Hall Garage and buy a
used car.

The sand-colored Toyota Corolla hatchback with
200,000 miles on its odometer costs him $2,300, tags
included. Budge's inaugural spin is two blocks to a rental
agency on Main Street. Again, he has quick luck: a
bayfront cottage beside the public beach is available for
immediate occupancy. The lease is month to month plus a
security deposit, utilities excluded. He drives over to have
a look, likes it (deems it affordable), drives back, writes a
check, and is handed the key. He then backtracks along
Main Street to Bayside Foods, the town's only supermarket, to provision for cupboard and refrigerator, not omitting beer.

Lastly — and this is only three hours later — he
returns to the dock to collect Ragu and the pile of possessions she is guarding (actually, she's asleep). Somehow, it

all fits in the old Corolla, with a few items tied to the roof. Setting up his new quarters, he suddenly remembers that he needs a bed. Bryden's Used Furniture ("Buy, Sell, Trade") on Route 20 has exactly what he is looking for: a double mattress and box spring that are not too tattered and not too stained. While he is on the premises, he also purchases a desk, a small table, and two chairs. These fit easily within the hatchback. Having lashed the mattress and box spring to the roof, he sets off once again for his new abode. In a matter of hours, then, his move is complete. To celebrate, he gets blitzed on the six-pack.

Chapter 2

The mosquitoes are bad here. Stepping outdoors is an invitation to a feast of blood — their feast, my blood. The best defense consists of long sleeves, jeans, and an aerosol repellent which I'm loath to use because it contains DEET. Overexposure to DEET can cause neurological damage, I'm told, and certain mosquitoes on Maryland's eastern shore carry West Nile virus, which is potentially fatal. Either way, the risks are probably slight, and so I take my chances. I've made up my mind not to die here, but if I do, I hope it won't be because of a mosquito bite.

In the sweltering room with the direct view of Chesapeake Bay beyond the beach portajohn, Budge is word-processing. The evergreen sap of creativity flows as always, despite his fallen circumstances. He has a compelling reason to hustle at the keyboard; his only chance for redemption, nay, survival, is to produce another book. Wisely or unwisely, he has chosen to write about himself, then cloak the autobiographical details in fiction. At the moment he has neither the time nor imagination to invent an interesting central character, so he himself will be the object of scrutiny. Given the reading public's appetite for odd cases of human misery, he knows he has nothing to lose.

I've parked myself and my worldly possessions within the walls of this cinderblock cottage. Beyond its back yard, a blowsy fringe of phragmites and cattails borders the breeze-rippled shallows. In the front yard, a boxwood

14

and willow oak compete for sunlight filtering through a grove of locust trees. Near the road is a protruding well cover made of pressed stone. A silver mailbox, a faded yellow fire hydrant, and a creosote-oozing utility pole complete the arrangement. My nearest neighbor is anybody who uses the portajohn at the corner of the public beach. I myself can urinate outdoors at night if I choose.

Although the view of the bay is panoramic, the beach itself isn't much to look at. About 400 feet long, it is a mostly grassy crescent of trucked-in sand. Just offshore, three rip-rap breakwaters insure that this sand isn't displaced by storms. People arrive en masse on the weekends, although few will venture in the water now that it is late July (dry weather brings increased salinity from the ocean, causing stinging nettles to migrate up the estuary). Directly inland, Beach Road widens for parking along a short boardwalk with five fixed benches. Two kiosks and three picnic tables (one right next to my cottage) are interspersed along the verge. A two-posted sign announces that the beach is closed from dusk till dawn, there's no lifeguard, and neither dogs nor alcoholic beverages are allowed — plus a number of other sensible rules, all of which are routinely broken.

Budge is embarrassed to admit, even to himself, that his professional track record has been spotty. He hasn't published a new book in seven years. Within the past fifteen months, he has had a magazine article in print (which he had to fight for, then suffer the humiliation of having it edited to oblivion), and several book signings (his entourage, that is to say, his wife and whichever of her relatives happened to be visiting, was larger than his audience), but mainly he's had a streak of unpublished writing. He's tried and tried and tried and tried. He used to be nearly famous, but now he is nearly unknown, and he resents the difference.

He has been thinking that possibly his marriage has had something to do with it. For his wife's sake, he may have tried too hard. Not that she goaded him or anything, but there was an understanding between them at the start of their marriage that he was earmarked for literary fortune. She said she believed in his talent. She said she loved him for being an established author. The fact that his career didn't follow the prescribed game plan, but instead petered out in a series of rejection slips hurt her more than it hurt him. While he was determined to plunk himself down in front of the computer screen and try again, she lost faith in his wordsmithing. Could he blame her? Yes, goddammit, he could. Whatever happened to *for better and for worse*? She began urging him to think about another career — real estate, social work, teaching ("You'd be great in the classroom, Budgie."), even housepainting — anything to increase his contribution to their finances.

Budge was genuinely puzzled. Didn't she know that an old dog can't learn new tricks? Why, most of their contemporaries were segueing into retirement or embarking on related second careers just to keep themselves active and useful. And yes, that's how he described himself to her: a trustworthy, highly specialized old hound, whose nose pointed irreversibly toward the scent of literature. Budge wouldn't budge; he didn't want another career. He believed in himself and that chimera called a lucky break. He would keep plugging away. They had a nice home — it wasn't a palace, but it suited their needs. They had a little spending money — not enough for exotic cruises, but enough for budget-minded getaways now and then. They had their health, their careers, their hobbies, their friendships.

"*You* take a better paying job, if you're so concerned about money," he'd tell her, and he'd launch into an oft-cited homily about how she knew from the start that she was marrying an artistic person.

"I'm not demanding that you stop being artistic," she'd retort. "I'm just asking you to bring in a little more money — *any*thing!"

He knew he was letting her down, and it gave him a sick feeling.

"Tell you what," he'd say (he said it at least five times previously). "Just let me finish this manuscript. I'll be done in six months. I promise you, this one will hit the charts. And if it doesn't, I'll go out and get a job."

But she'd heard it all before. She simply didn't believe him anymore. At this point, all the rote optimism had gone sour. She wanted a spouse who was more financially dependable and capable of career flexibility. He likened himself to a ship with a stuck rudder. He was congenitally unable to change his course. It chilled him to realize he loved his wife more than she loved him.

Newly arrived in Rock Hall, he has had a little time to think all this over. It *was* his love for her that made him expect too much of himself. He watched her change from muse to tormentor. At first she offered gentle encouragement — she was a crackerjack proofreader, too — but when the long dry spell showed no sign of letting up, it became clear that she could not have cared less what he was writing. His most recent undertaking, about the Boer War, she called his "vanity book." She was supporting the project financially, she minced no words. She had no expectations whatsoever for its success, and this time she wasn't going to wait around to prove that she was right.

Chained to his computer screen day and night, typing till his wrists ached and his eyes glazed over, reshuffling the research notes and chapter outlines, asking her to wait a little longer and promising that he had a true bestseller in the works — none of it meant anything to her. She lost all sympathy. She told him he was using her — and not only using her, but abusing her as well. Angry words were exchanged.

Insidiously, a new kind of communication sprang up between us: we argued. Our differences weren't momentous; in fact, they were usually about nothing at all, but somehow we'd get on opposite viewpoints of the most picayune subjects, and proceed to hold forth mercilessly, as though winning debate points off each other was a matter of life or death. Now she and I became short-fused and easily offended — it wasn't always that way — and we developed the knack for sticking the dagger of insult just where it hurt the most. I began to dread the swooping vehemence of our disagreements. Most of the time, we functioned as a like-minded couple, seasoned to each other's idiosyncrasies — in a word, durable. We could practically read each other's thoughts. But after a truce of several day's duration, there'd come the inevitable flare-up. I'd blame her and she'd blame me, and we'd fall into the same old destructive pattern — arguing for argument's sake. Of course we always made up, even when our arguments lasted into the night and continued the next morning, but the inevitability of verbal discord began to redefine the way we related to each other. I grew wary of saying what was on my mind, and I'm sure she did too. The wrong comment, even the mildest of observations, could trigger a fresh altercation. As she facetiously put it, we were overcommunicating.

In his lonely leisure, Budge writes these words. Try as

18

he might, he can only remember his wife with love. He can't help himself; he has every reason in the world to hate her, but his emotions aren't wired that way. Even remembering her most stinging put-downs doesn't do the trick. If he could only hate her a little bit, he'd be farther along the road to recovery, he tells himself. It has been well over ninety days since she walked out and he still loves her as much as the day they got married.

But can two highly verbal spouses stop talking to each other? Well, that became a problem in itself. Our silences were dangerous; noncommunication could mean that the one or the other was stewing, fomenting, withdrawing affection or — worst — getting ready to explode. Stalking separately around the house, passing each other in a room without making eye contact — it was a lousy way to live as husband and wife. The cessation of conversation seemed unnatural for two gifted talkers who shared the rapport we did. During such silences I harbored intense feelings of insecurity. What had I said or done to offend her this time? Would she stop making love with me? One summer we crossed Canada by car, and what I remember mostly from that trip, aside from the sightseeing high-lights, was the arguing and the crushing feeling of inade-quacy that grew within me as we got farther from home. We couldn't agree on anything. My itinerary suggestions, reasonable as they were, irked her. Something within me, in my personality provoked her. Being myself, loving and wanting her as I did, only pushed her farther away. Everything I offered, everything I contributed seemed to end with a question mark.

There will be no more trips for a long time, save trips to the grocery store and the gas station. Plastic, i.e., credit card nonchalance is over; the surety of his wife's paycheck is a thing of the past. His health insurance (under her group plan) is expired. Book royalties have dwindled to next to nothing. Before he sold the boat, he sold a raft of possessions, including his motorcycle, his saxophone, his power tools and gardening equipment, plus several pieces of antique furniture that had belonged to his great-grandmother. The divorce lawyer demanded a retainer as large as a typical book advance (typical for a writer like Budge Moss, that is).

So despite his love for his wife, Budge is scraping the bottom of the barrel, thanks to her. This can cause him to write with bitterness.

Somehow, as a result of my confused emotions, I ignored the larger picture, i.e., the marriage itself, which I assumed would remain intact. Because I cherished my wife and couldn't be other than completely faithful to her, I trusted her to hold me in the same esteem. We were in a committed relationship; our transient lows were always matched by transient highs. So we argued — every couple argues, I reasoned. Maybe we argued a bit more than other couples — it was just our way of letting off steam. Did we need counseling? Nah, it wasn't that serious. One look at the stupid stuff we argued about made it plain: we had a minor league problem that would disappear over time.

Budge sits at his desk and looks out at the bay. Love has a beginning and an end, he muses, just like everything else. His love for his estranged wife will end, but he doesn't have a clue as to when and how. It hasn't been an easy year. He knows he shouldn't be too hard on himself.

And then the events of September 11th occurred, which seemed to cast both a truce and a pall upon our relationship. My wife was at work that morning and called to tell me to turn on the television. Separately, we watched the jetliners strike, the thunderheads of burning fuel, the fragments and people falling, then the towers collapse. Frequent visitors to the city, we were stunned to see the skyline thus reduced. She came home early and we watched more of the coverage. Then, entwined naked on the bed as if we were survivors, we acting out a sad but reaffirmative grappling of grief.

For days afterwards, we were both too traumatized and self-absorbed to argue. Three weeks, maybe four weeks went by on the evenest of marital keels. But then we had an argument in which she actually broke down and cried — a rare occurrence for an arguer of her stature. It floored me to see that I had penetrated beyond the bulldog of her intellect; I had actually hurt her. All the times I felt like crying and never did — well, here she was one-upping me, baring her pain as I had never been able to. Argument-wise, she always gave as good or better than she got, but now, for the first time, she was defeated. All of a sudden, I realized that I had gotten so used to perceiving myself as victim — the bested obliger, the patient sufferer — that I neglected to see how she was as much a victim of our disagreements as I.

He gets up to retrieve a beer from the refrigerator. Directly outside the window, not fifty feet away, a party of four has arrived with a cooler and a tote of picnic supplies. A nuclear family, two adults and two kids, so casually ensconced in their roles — will-o'-the-wisps, he thinks — bearing their normality as if it were a birthright. Budge Moss, solitary single writer, soon to be divorced, looks up from the screen and takes a long pull from the bottle.

At the start of the new year, our marriage changed. My wife did something she had never done before: she started bullshitting me. I had always admired her for her directness and honesty; now I felt that she wasn't dealing me straight. Most of the time she was, of course, but every once in a while, I could tell — just by the inflection in her voice — that she was conning me, pulling the wool over my eyes. She began spending one night a week away from home on the pretext that her commute was too long (I fully sympathized — she drove fifty miles). At social gatherings, she flirted with other men (at first it was a turn-on, watching my wife act sexy). Our credit card bills showed charges that she refused to explain (hey, it was her money). Reluctantly, I took it all in stride.

Budge remembers how this was when she decided she wanted to move to New York City. The announcement came out of the blue: she thought it might be best if they lived apart for a while. And she didn't want to live just anywhere in Manhattan; she wanted to live in Battery Park City, in the shadow of the recent devastation. "I want to give something back," she said. "I feel as if I belong there at this point in my life. You can join me on weekends if you wish."

It was not an invitation. It was a strange mental mechanism that linked her to the aftermath of the terrorism, an identification that reportedly was quite common in those days. She would join the crowd at Ground Zero and take part in rebuilding the community. My presence was immaterial. A weekend husband? How long would that last? She'd pare down my presence to a weekend a month, then none at all. It was just her way of breaking the news gently — only it hit me like a ton of bricks. Like a skyscraper falling.

With a snort of hindsight, Budge recalls the marital denouement over the weeks that followed. There was some talk of him moving upstate, not more than an hour by rail — the greater Poughkeepsie area, say — and taking the train into the city to visit her. She encouraged him to check out Kingston, New Paltz, Rhinebeck, Red Hook. He did as she asked him, but came back unmoved. For his part, he tried to talk her out of lower Manhattan, mentioning the rents, the noise, the crime, the particulate matter that was injurious to the lungs, the inconvenience of schlepping groceries. She scoffed at what she termed his paranoia. He then urged marriage counseling — something he had heretofore been too manly to consider. He spoke with utmost sincerity: her medical plan covered a certain number of counseling sessions, so maybe now was the time to avail themselves of this service. She declined joint counseling, but added that if he wanted to get some for himself, it was fine with her. He got mad at her for saying that and told her to go fuck herself.

She slept in the guest bedroom for a couple of days, but came back on my birthday. She undressed in the dark, and lay down on her side of the bed without the slightest remonstrance of interest in what was about to transpire between us. She wasn't cold or stiffened in body, but she had turned off her mind. Her flesh was yielding and pliant, warm and scented as always, replete with its secrets and detours and rewards as it had ever been. She let me touch and caress her at will. With lips and fingertips, I explored every facet of her voluptuous supine stature. Her passivity aroused me to thunderous pitch. My blood boiled like I

23

had the bends. At the moment for entering her, she parted her legs with a tired willingness that made me reflect on the thousands of times we had had sex together. Skip the love, focus on the sex. This woman I knew so completely, so intimately, was offering herself as a specimen of what I would be physically missing — and she knew what she was doing and was in full control. There in the darkness, her attitude was unmistakable. As I moved within her and we rocked together toward the completion of our coital prerogative, I felt her detachment. She was way ahead of me; I was still luxuriating in our marriage, but she was already getting over it.

It was pretty much upstairs/downstairs sleeping arrangements after that, although she did join me every few days in that same fashion. It nearly drove me crazy.

Budge pauses here to masturbate. He has taken up the habit lately, though it seems wholly undignified for a man of 55 to need such urgent relief. He walks into the cottage's bedroom, lowers his shorts, lies on his back (sandals and shirt still on) and gets it over with quickly. His climax is scientific, not sensual. Far in the back of his mind is a tinge of adolescent guilt; he hasn't done this in years, he hasn't had to do it on a regular basis since he was in the Peace Corps back in the 1970s.

Then, one Saturday morning, not a week after Easter, she moved out. I was at the supermarket, buying groceries for the two of us, and when I went through the checkout, my credit card was declined. "Your account is closed," said the clerk.

I pretended to be unconcerned. Thumbing through my wallet, I handed her another card. "Here, try this one."

"I'm sorry, sir, this account is closed, too."

24

She looked at me with suspicious eyes. I did my best to conceal my shock, mumbling something about how the bank must've screwed up and I'd look into the matter right away. I didn't have my checkbook, I didn't have enough cash. Other customers were queued behind me; their impatience was mounting. The clerk exhaled sharply, as if to say, "What the hell are you gonna do now?"

I was so embarrassed that I momentarily froze. We all stood there — the guilty party, the inquisitor, and the irritated onlookers, several of whom were shunting to alternate checkout lanes. Finally, I mustered the courage to fake it. "Would you set these aside for me, please?" I asked. "I'll go to the bank and get this straightened out."

Looking out at the portajohn and the water beyond, Budge remembers how he went right home. He knew he had to confront his wife immediately, do his utmost to pull her back from the brink before it was too late. If they couldn't do some serious talking now, their whole world would fall apart.

But when he arrived home, three cars were backed up on the lawn with their doors and trunks open. She had enlisted helpers and was already in the process! Besides embarrassment, he now felt humiliation; she had robbed him of his dignity. She hadn't even had the decency to warn him.

I cornered her in the kitchen as she was packing up her silverware. "What are you doing?" I asked angrily.

"It should be pretty obvious what I'm doing."

"Why are you doing this?"

"Because it's not working out between us. It's over."

"Where are you going?"

"None of your business."

Oh, she was seething and unapproachable. If she had a pang of regret or remorse, she didn't show it. Our endgame, with its intermittent sexual favors, was finished. She had evidently played the last straw; she would no longer suffer my presence. Now my entreaties were altogether in vain. It was as if I was speaking to her in a language she no longer understood.

Budge looks out at the bay, shaking his head. A punctured married life collapses quickly. She didn't give him her new phone number. She'd talk business with him only by e-mail. They agreed that she would keep the car and he would keep the boat. They agreed to put their house up for sale and he'd live in it until it sold, although with two mortgages and some personal debt, there'd be no payoff to speak of. Fortunately, the real estate market was booming; the house went under contract within two weeks. Budge had 60 days to straighten out his affairs. What he didn't sell or simply throw out, he moved to the boat. Coincidentally, he started getting interested in Rock Hall — the idea of it, the idea of arriving by water and beginning a new life.

Now he is transplanted, lonely, low on cash, inspired to write of his grief, and forcibly getting used to his new surroundings.

Chapter 3

Faux rock cinderblock originated in the 1920s, when the molded replication of chiseled granite was thought to be more visually arresting than the mundane block itself. Nowadays, faux rock looks cheesy; it's artificiality offends the eye. It's clearly not what it pretends to be. Its rough-hewn surface accumulates grime that accentuates the industrial fakery. Moreover, I've learned from past experience that cinderblock dwellings, as a rule, lack insulation. Come wintertime, I may rue the faux rock for practical as well as aesthetic reasons.

But it's a stout cottage — that can't be denied. It won't fall down anytime soon. Its asphalt shingled roof peaks steeply on all four sides, the eaves gutterless (thus accounting for the dirt penumbra along the bottom two feet of wall). The interior consists of a living room, two small bedrooms, a bathroom, and a kitchen in which a stacked washer and dryer take up half the floor space. Countertop and cabinets are booby trapped with poison bait for cockroaches, ants, and mice. The other night, I had to deal with a bat flying through a hole in the ceiling that I subsequently sealed with duct tape. Window sashes need to be propped open with sticks, the screening's useless. I've placed a fly swatter in each room. After a fashion, everything works.

Budge is off to a good start, although he won't admit it. If he weren't feeling so sorry for himself, he'd see that he has landed on his feet with his health, his sanity, his necessary possessions, and his pet (who is taking to the new digs with feline aplomb). What Budge doesn't have now is a wife who was going to leave him sooner or later.

Yet despite a marital past far more rocky than rosy, he pines for the life he left behind — the big house, the social calendar, the lawn he cared for as if it mattered deeply in the great scheme of things, the no-limit shopping. He misses the big car with its leather interior and cloud-like suspension. He misses the lineup of tools and leisure toys along the walls of his garage. He misses the whine of the heat pump compressor concealed within the privet. He misses the neighbors who confirmed his existence with lives that closely mimicked his own, bracketing him with barbecue smells and barking dogs and pool-splashing squeals of delight and leaves to be raked (or blown) as they dropped off the well-pruned trees, and so on throughout the suburban infinitum.

Then, too, he misses his wife – even the least aspect about her, like the way she put the laundry in the dryer and emptied the dishwasher. The way she arrived home late in the afternoon, sometimes too exhausted to do anything for the first half hour but sit down with the newspaper and a reheated cup of coffee. She did work hard, he'll give her credit for that. Financially, she kept them going. But he worked hard also; many nights after supper he returned to his desk for two or three hours.

With morose clarity, he remembers the good times they had. The big trips and little trips. The parties, theirs and others'. The many cultural events they attended, the movies they saw. The restaurants they dined in enough times to refer to as "favorites." And the galaxy of goings-on they shared in the bedroom: dressing and undressing, solving crossword puzzles, watching DVD movies, reading news magazines to each other, and — always lastly — making love. Foreplay, wordplay, replay — he can't get the memories out of his brain.

It's all gone, he reminds himself. The pining is pointless. Healing hasn't just begun; it started on the day she walked out, which is over three months ago.

Budge struggles to adjust his mind to the current reality. He's come to a place as good as any and a lot better than some. A waterman's hamlet since the early 1800s, Rock Hall is an incorporated town situated between a series of coves called necks. It's contemporary trade and traffic, geared toward tourism and pleasure boating, includes seven marinas offering hundreds upon hundreds of boat slips, six charter fishing services, five motels, four B&Bs, nine restaurants, three bars, an old-time soda fountain, a fudge shop, two historical museums, six or seven emporia specializing in antiques and crafts (the number fluctuates), and four realty agencies. From the picturesque rubber-tired trolley, all this was fresh and captivating when he first arrived. Already, the novelty is wearing off.

That damn trolley passes right in front of the cottage — ding! ding! — after discharging and picking up beachgoers. I have no cause to complain or be critical, but it can be annoying at times. I find myself wishing I were a tourist, a carefree half of a couple sashaying through town, laughing, spending money freely, surfeited with delight. Instead, I'm a penny-pinching renter peering through my screen door — never to ride, always to watch.

Come wintertime, the northeasterly winds off the bay will blow the tides lower, the shops will close, the boats will be propped on dry land, and the tourists will go home. Rock Hall will contract to its locals-only self, a grid of modest homes behind mailboxes and manicured lawns.

But winter is a long way off right now. Adjacent to the

cottage, the beach is crowded, and Budge can't help but eavesdrop. A party of municipal boosters — town councilmen? — has gathered at the nearest kiosk, and they're bragging about how Rock Hall is destined for an infrastructural explosion along the lines of Oxford and St. Michaels, given another ten years or so and a chugging economy. Could this really come to pass? Budge doubts it, recollecting information gleaned from his Internet research. Twelve miles to the north is Chestertown — a niche destination of greater historical appeal, despite the fact that George Washington is said to have been ferried to Rock Hall no fewer than five times (on his way to Chestertown, it must be admitted). Chestertown's population hasn't changed significantly in 300 years, but change comes even more slowly to this nether end of Kent County. Proposed developments are battled strenuously and usually defeated. People resist the future here; they like things the way they are. Small town life on the eastern shore is based on the assumption that what's here today will be here tomorrow.

But what does he know? He is a stranger to the locale; his perceptions are warped, to say the least. He is floating free of everything that held him down before. He could be sitting at his desk, typing away at the computer, and *poof!*, cardiac arrest could wipe him out of existence (God's flyswatter). Who'd miss him then? Not a damn soul. His parents: dead. His closest relatives: five states away. His friends: ha! what friends? His e-mail pals would assume he was out of town. When the rent came due, there might be an investigation into his whereabouts, but until then, *nada*.

Do people implode when they have nothing or nobody to live for, he wonders? Do they just shrivel up and grow strange, relying on so-called inner strength to pull them into old age, at which point they disappear from society's radar? Will he be walking at the edge of the highway while the luckier ones rocket past?

With loneliness, Budge grows philosophical. He has been here only a few days, yet he is quite at a loss as to how to proceed. For several months now, he has fallen into the habit of talking to himself, or more specifically, talking to his estranged wife. Peering through a window at the throng on the beach, he starts doing it again.

"Do you have any idea what you've reduced me to? Do you realize how traumatizing it is to be treated like that? What you did and the way you did it — I just can't get over it. How could you hold me in such low esteem? I was your husband, for chrissake."

Halting in mid-sentence, he excoriates himself loud and clear. "Stop this stupid shit right now, Budge Moss! Stop talking to her!"

And he'll stop for a few minutes, maybe even an hour or more, as he turns his mind to other matters. He'll sit in the yard with Ragu and read last Sunday's paper. He'll attempt a crossword puzzle. He'll whittle down his stack of subscription magazines (more should be forwarded to the new address any day now). He'll pare his fingernails and toenails if he has nothing better to do. And because he's a seasoned pro, it's always fairly effortless for him to return to his métier.

Rock Hall is the anchor to which the chain of my existence is now attached — a chain of gossamer, it seems, that connects the tatters of my old life to one yet to be lived. Beach Road is the bay floor; I will sink no lower. I'm here for the duration, whatever that entails, so it's up to me to muster the courage. Being sunk, now I must learn to swim. I know what I'm supposed to do next: meet peo-

ple. Yes, walk right up to 'em and smile. Interact, social-ize, get a life, show what a nice normal friendly guy I am.

He's got the right idea, but implementation is no piece of cake. Heartsick thoughts worm their way into his conscious mind. Before he knows it, he has slipped into another imaginary scenario: his estranged wife is e-mailing him. Clearly, she is thawing; she may want him back.

Thanks for your latest. I've been having second thoughts as well. I know you're lonely (believe me, I'm lonely too), but I felt I had no choice other than to break away when I did. Cheers,

And another:

Am mailing a check to cover your expenses for hiring the truck to take the stuff I left behind to the landfill. I trust it'll cover some of your labor, too, which I greatly appreciate. Wish I could pay more, but funds are tight with me right now, too. Cheers,

Oh, he could invent them all day long. They pop into his head, one after the other, each an explanation, a query, an apology, a link in the chain between estrangement and reconciliation.

Let me tell you, some days I look back and think that we both went temporarily insane. Just what exactly are you doing with yourself these days? And how do you like Rock Hall? Cheers,

In his mind, he has proffered an invitation, and her imaginary response thrills him to no end.

Dinner on Sunday at your place sounds great. Please give directions. How about if I bring one of your favorite desserts (a surprise for now)? Cheers,

His favorite dessert, he thinks, would be served in bed: the human éclair.

That was nice of you to invite me for margaritas on the beach. I'd love to come — can I get back to you after I check my calendar? Cheers,

His problem is that he can't stop. On and on his fancy flies. She is not exactly begging to take him back, but he knows her well enough to see the possibilities in her nuance. She is being coy; she just needs a little more time alone. Eventually, she'll come to her senses, and when she does, she'll adore him more than ever.

This pleasant reverie continues as he washes the dishes and empties the garbage. It occupies his mind as he e-mails his buddies and checks the latest Ebay offerings. It may even go on while he brushes and flosses. Then, at some point, he figuratively smacks himself across the mouth. Cut this crap out! Quit this asinine pipedream *now*! She is not coming back. She has given you absolutely no indication that she is. She is gone, man, *gone*! Do you understand what that means? G-O-N-E, gone, like the wind. She's made a complete break, she wants nothing to do with you anymore. You had some good years together, but they're over, and you've got to move on. M-O-V-E O-N. Make more of an effort to meet people. Work harder to make new friends. You're single again, revel in it! Stop thinking of yourself as an old soon-to-be divorced duffer. This celibate life is pointless. You're too old to be jerking off! Forget the comfy conjugal memories — get out there and prove that you can still cut the mustard!

Thus Budge takes himself to task. His mandate is simple enough. In two words: get laid. The sheer sexual relief — the real McCoy — would take the edge off his bitterness, dilute the residue of his humiliation. But no, it's more complicated than that. He needs to restore his old confidence, a phoenix from the ashes. His coordinates can no longer be planted in the past. He must honestly say, "I've gotten beyond all that and now I need to reach out." Only when he does this will his new life proceed where the old one went kaput.

This is another reason why I chose the cottage by the beach: the opportunity to make new friends. But believe me, it's taking some effort to crawl out of my shell! My first impulse has been to hold myself aloof from the beachgoers. But a week has gone by; I see the disadvantages to that strategy. Therefore, I resolve to spend more time outdoors.

One of the beach's primary functions, Budge learns, is a place to observe sunsets. A group of locals calling themselves the Sunset Club congregates on the boardwalk benches every evening. Mostly retirees, they're a convivial bunch whose conversation regularly expands upon the whys and wherefors of Rock Hall politics. As a newcomer to the neighborhood, Budge is invited to sit and join in, although his presence tends to skew the topic of conversation. Self identified as a writer and single man, he is a bona fide curiosity — a topic in his own right.

These folks arrive half an hour before the bright raspberry orb drops behind the western shore, and stay until dusk when no mosquito repellent, brand-name or home-

*concocted, is strong enough to ward off the bloodsucking
buzz bombers. With hurried farewells and slaps to bare
skin, the group disperses. Only the people who've stayed
in their vehicles with motors running and windows rolled
up can hang around with impunity.*

*Bidding my own adieus and smacking my own welts, I
walk the few steps homeward. A drainage ditch (a breed-
ing ground?) separates the beach from my yard, and I
choose to jump over it rather than get my feet wet. My little cat is there to greet me; she appears to have no interest in the world beyond the drainage ditch, which will be
— it is hoped — a factor in her continued longevity.*

Mornings at the beach offer a very different dynamic.
There is usually nobody in sight until ten o'clock, when
the weekend and weekly renters wander outdoors with
their coffee cups. Two such transients always catch
Budge's eye — a pair of middle-aged women in bikinis.
They stand — oiled, deeply tanned, their flesh gone slack
though still appealing— on the lawn of the first cottage on
the far side of the strand. One is a brunette, the other is a
frosted blonde. They just stand there, smoking and drink-
ing — evidently something harder than coffee — all
morning, all afternoon. Sometimes there is a man with
them.

*What keeps me from making their acquaintance? It
would be the neighborly thing to do — casually stroll over
and introduce myself. One of them is surely single and, by
the looks of her, ready for some kind of action. It might be
a quick solution to my ridiculous celibacy.*

*But I quake at the thought of putting on a macho bon-
homie act and running the risk of success. First of all, neither woman has that je-ne-sais-quoi. The vacuity of their*

never-changing stance is a turn-off. If one of them had a book or a magazine in her hands, I might think otherwise. But all they're holding, all they ever hold, are cigarettes and (presumably) highballs.

Second, neither appears as though she could offer sensitivity on the level I seek. I'm extrapolating here (and might be way off base), but there's something in their sagging copper abdomens and Day-Glo busts, exposed for all the world to ogle, that predicates a hardness of mind. (I can be tough as nails myself, but only in the cause of defensiveness.) These women look like they're telling the world to fuck off. I'm hesitant to come under their evaluating gaze. Besides, my heart has standards, damn it! I'm still too deep in the sex equals love equation. I guess I've done it that way too long.

Thus he excuses himself from committing to substantive action. If the women are looking across the beach at him, they might be thinking, *what a standoffish prick! Every day he's staring out the window at us. Wonder what his problem is?*

Oh, he's off to a great start all right — turning down one promising scenario after another. Lots of single women come to the beach — to sunbathe, wade, walk their dogs, hang out with friends. What does he do? He watches them as he formulates intellectual and aesthetic excuses for keeping his distance. If only he could get over what ails him! Lower the bar, drop his reserve, ignore the hurt that keeps waving a red flag in his face.

He understands his problem and knows the havoc it is causing — this state of mind that constantly references the comforts of the past. It makes the present unappetizing, negates it almost. And yet the loudspeaker of his conscience barks in his ear: *will the real Budge Moss please come to the claims counter and reclaim his life? And while he's at it, will he at least make an attempt to rid himself of unnecessary baggage?*

This is how the first few weeks in the cottage pass — a lonely man mostly keeping his own company, venturing only as far as the boardwalk benches to socialize at sunset. He knows he's got to make more of an effort – he has promised himself that, and he always keeps his promises to himself — but the details haven't been worked out yet. Most of the time, he is still conversing with the beloved object who is no longer his own and never will be. Every night he dreams of her. By day, he has perfected the art of chastising her unavailable ears.

If you'd only listened to me! We didn't have to end it this way. We didn't have to end it at all. We could have gotten some counseling and worked out our differences. You could have aired your grievances, instead of clamming up the way you did. Do you realize that I still have no idea why you left?

And:

I haven't asked you this question before, but I'll ask it now: what did you find so repulsive in me that made you flee my presence? Was it some monstrous flaw in my character? Was it some terrible deed you thought I was about to commit?

Objectively speaking, what makes a woman like you run away from a man like me? To be frank, I can't see that much wrong with me. I know I burp and fart and leave the toilet seat up and forget birthdays and anniversaries. I know that when I take off my shoes, they drop to the floor in a way that annoys you. I know I like plenty of sex — too much, as you claim — and am not the greatest human weathervane (or barometer) when you're not in the mood. But aside from these, where else am I so majorly deficient? Hasn't the constancy of my love brought you happiness? Hasn't my appreciation for your beauty and intelligence made you feel secure?

And the classic:

At this point, if you want me back, you're going to have to beg. I mean really beg — get down on your knees and grovel. I've suffered miserably because of you. I've lost sleep, lost possessions, lost my home, and damn near lost my bearings. True, my love for you goes on and on, but that doesn't mean I'm "easy." You've done me a great wrong; my faith in you is shattered. But if you take me back right away — like tomorrow, if not tonight — I'm prepared to let bygones be bygones.

Chapter 4

By the middle of August, after Budge has been in Rock Hall for just over a month, he is finally making some headway. He has sold a feature article to *The Washington Post* (*"Living the Laid-back Life on Maryland's Eastern Shore"*). He has gotten another credit card — he can walk down the aisles of Bayside Foods without hanging his head and fearing a relapse of post-traumatic stress disorder. He has struck up conversation with habitués at the post office and the pharmacy. He has attended a parade, a boat exhibition, a public hearing, and a fishing contest. In addition, he has met many of the neighbors along Beach Road.

Also, he has started going to Friday potluck suppers at the Mainstay, a nonprofit storefront on Main Street that doubles as an art gallery and concert venue. Budge discovers the suppers quite by accident. Late one Friday afternoon when he's driving past the Mainstay, he notices its signboard advertising a local jazz trio. On a whim, he decides to attend, so he heads home and undertakes no small effort to make himself presentable. He trims his beard, dons a clean shirt and slacks, puts ticket money in his pocket, and times his arrival just right, only to discover that he has come on the wrong night.

He walks in just as the potluck is winding down. Twenty people seemingly greet him all at once; he is vociferously encouraged to grab a Styrofoam plate and take whatever food is left — a chicken drumstick, a cold pizza slice, a helping of tuna casserole (plenty of that), a caved-in wedge of white potato pie. Hungrily, Budge devours the plateful. Unfortunately, the wine is all gone.

Somebody asks where he lives. Between chewed mouthfuls, he mentions the cottage on Beach Road and that he has only recently moved to town. Revealing these facts results in a deluge of polite inquisitiveness. His listeners appear to hang on his every word.

Are they smitten by my engaging personality, my charming smile, my svelte physique, or just the novelty of my presence? When I tell them I'm an author, they ask the obvious follow-ups, but it turns out that not a single one of them has ever heard of me, much less read my books. Perhaps I should introduce myself as James A. Michener.

Amid the sociable clusters of coupledom are two or three single women who Budge zeroes in on. One is a math teacher from Philadelphia, a skinny woman in a sun dress, with a face like an English walnut and blue veins running every which way on her chest. She's younger than he is, perhaps in her late forties, yet her eyes evaluate him with a candor that can only have come from much practice. She proceeds to tell him about the benefits of her singles tennis club — strongly hinting that he should join — but he can't get a word in edgewise, so he listens to her for fifteen minutes before excusing himself to get another helping of casserole. He turns to another woman, this one in jeans and a designer sweatshirt, somewhat older and fairly good-looking, but her voice and attention keep trailing off as she glances anxiously around the room. Mumbling some excuse, she slips away during one such hiatus.

A third woman — of indeterminate age — in a garish dashiki shows a more balanced conviviality. Her name is Teresa Potter; she is a weaver who has recently moved to

Rock Hall (it turns out she lives just down the road from him). She is not physically appealing — pear-shaped, plum-faced, peach-topped — but she has a nice personality. Her previous address was Santa Fe, New Mexico.

"I don't care what anybody tells you about the health benefits of dwelling in the southwest," she tells him. "The air's so dry that after a while, you can hardly breathe anymore."

Teresa is in the process of unpacking and setting up her loom. As she describes the procedure, he studies her in detail. Her hair — more the color of pink champagne, he concludes — seems grossly affected by static electricity. Her complexion is egregiously freckled. Her earlobes sag with complex earrings. Around her neck hangs a silver pendant that is larger than a medallion but smaller than a bicycle sprocket. She is shod in cordovan mules that make her feet resemble hooves.

While avoiding a direct look into her eyes, he notes that her bifocal frames are the most curvaceous thing about her. He also notices her mannish wristwatch and the lumpy backs of her stubby hands. Artsy rings encircle at least five of her fingers. But all in all, she is a calm, unpretentious person. He begins to see the possibilities in her.

So this is what single folks do, I'm thinking to myself. Check 'em over visually as you pretend to be listening. Tot up the positives and negatives, and if something overwhelms you either way, make a point to study it at leisure. Teresa's flaws aren't anything that time run backward couldn't erase. What I mean to say is there are no outward deficiencies in her personality. Nor is she that hard to look at, I conclude — it's all a matter of adjustment. So I decide to pursue her for a while just to see what she's like.

41

A week later, Budge has chatted with her twice on the phone and arranged to meet her again at the Friday pot luck. A cheap date, he figures, and this way he can veer off to other prospects when and if the conversation lags. He's bringing a bowl of tabouli replete with fresh tomatoes and parsley and a serving spoon. He asked her what she was bringing, but she didn't know.

The crowd is larger, maybe twice that of the previous potluck. Budge's first impression is that there'll be plenty of other women to talk to. He heads straight for the buffet table, setting his contribution between a platter of deviled eggs and a salver of brown chunks in gravy that turns out to be goatmeat. Recognizing at least ten friendly faces, he begins to socialize without hesitation (he has always been good at remembering names — a holdover from his book-signing days).

Ten, fifteen minutes go by with no sign of Teresa. Mindful that the offerings are quickly running out, he grabs a plate and fork and commences to load up, not omitting his own delectable contribution and somebody else's wine. Following this, he bravely barges into a con-vocation of complete strangers, taking an empty chair and authoritatively introducing himself.

No wallflower am I tonight! My goal is to make Budge Moss a household word in Rock Hall.

Perhaps Teresa has decided not to come after all. Well, it's her loss. Systematically, Budge plies conversa-tion with every female face that confronts him. Age and looks and marital status don't matter; he glides free and easy on myriad topics, garnering and giving laughter, drip-ping with attentiveness, drenched in sincerity, surpressing any inclination to be judgmental. He's just happy to have a square meal, a glassful of free merlot, and a chance to talk with other people. When he finally stands up for seconds — wine included — and dessert, he works his way across the room and sits with a different group. He is too full of energy and lightness of being to withhold himself from anybody who might seek the pleasure of his company.

Nearly an hour later, when he's mellowly talked out and stuffed to the point of bursting, in walks Teresa with a huge pot of baked beans. He's struck by how short and shapeless she is. Her peachy hairdo looks as if it has been wired to a Van de Graaff generator. She's got on a smear of lipstick, a little eye makeup, a ton of jewelry. Her purple shantung tunic distends above bellbottom trousers of the same tint, and the heavy beanpot is pressed against her chest like an offering that could spill over and ruin her finery in an instant. She has a quizzical, pained look on her face — she's realizing how late she is.

Out of pity, Budge goes over to relieve her of her burden, placing it on the table with the mostly polished-off platters and serving dishes.

I feel so sorry for her, truly I do. She probably lost track of time on my account, getting all gussied up and nervous and hoping for the best. And the beans! God, she's brought enough to feed an army! I imagine she'll be eating them at home for the next three weeks. There's something irregular and touching about her — she's so out of it! Among her skeins and spindles, she must live in her own little world — I haven't seen it firsthand, but I imagine it so. I feel terribly guilty for asking her to meet me here. It was all my idea and she couldn't say no.

Budge sits with her and does most of the talking while

43

she eats (predominantly beans). He can't tell if she is glad for his company or not; she is unfailingly polite, but she manifests no particular interest in pushing the envelope of their relationship, so to speak. As he prattles on about his writing, his cottage, his cat, his past and future, she listens, but that's about it. He starts to wonder if he is wasting his breath. Is she completely numb? Have her highs and lows been chemically flatlined?

As he talks, he can't help but give her the once-over again. Call it sexual scrutiny, call it incorrigible curiosity, it is a habit that Budge the writer and practiced observer of human nature falls into readily. A refrain of an old country song comes to his mind about how the girls always look prettier at closing time. Well, she's a girl, isn't she? And closing time's coming up, isn't it?

When she's finished eating, he proposes that she drop by his place on the pretext of showing her the cottage, showing her his books, showing her anything he's got that she might be interested in. She'll be, he tells her, his very first guest! He'll give her a ride, too. Indifferently, she assents. He volunteers to heft the beanpot to the parking lot, and she carries his near-empty tabouli dish and spoon.

Driving across town, Budge secretly congratulates himself. He has known her type before. They play the indifferent game all the way. It's a kind of old-fashioned-female existential position, not overtly wanting attention but not saying no to it either. In his horny state, it doesn't matter. With a little luck, he'll score.

In the cottage, he offers her a glass of wine.

She announces that she doesn't drink. "What, not even a glass of wine? How about a beer, then?"

"No, nothing at all, thanks. Alcohol doesn't agree with me."

44

"Fine," I say, "how about some tea? I've got herbal tea."

No, she doesn't want tea either, herbal or otherwise, nor decaf, nor even a glass of water.

"Is there anything you do want?" I ask, hinting as strongly as I dare.

No, she doesn't want anything. She arranges herself on the chair and just sits there. It takes me an arsenal of verbal gambits to wean her away from silence. Eventually, though, she consents to talk. At first we discuss the weather and upcoming events in Rock Hall, but her tongue loosens further when we get on the Single Person's Two Favorite Subjects: marriage and divorce.

She begins to open up now — don't we all? — as she outlines the downward graph of her 20-year marriage that ended ten years ago (her one and only matrimonial experience). Out of high school, she fell in love with a native of Greece, who turned out to be a habitual cheater. At times, he even lived outright with other women. Addicted to a cushy lifestyle and too cowed to venture out on her own, Teresa coped as best she could. Finally, her grown daughter convinced her to get a divorce and move in with her — a living arrangement that lasted for seven years until the teen-age grandchildren began overrunning the household. That was when Teresa fled to Santa Fe.

When Budge expresses disgust at her ex-husband's behavior, Teresa smiles blankly and says that she forgave him years ago. Furthermore, she adds that she communicates frequently with him in letters and phone calls — always has and always will. There are no hard feelings.

I want to ask, Why aren't there hard feelings? Why can't she show her anger? The Greek misused her, robbed her of self-confidence, circumscribed her life and filled decades of it with pain — and she forgives him?

As I study Teresa in the chair, I see what I missed earlier. She has a robotic quality about her, as if she's been trepanned by years of psychic abuse. Emotion has been wrung out of her; all that's left is a benign resignation, a shuffling along. She asks no questions and expects no answers.

I realize that my prospects for the evening have grown dim. My desire for her, nebulous as it is, has shrunk to zilch. This person has about as much interest in sex as a eunuch on saltpeter. She looks at her watch and announces — so like an old person looking at her watch and announcing! — that it's time to be walking home.

Budge offers to walk with her, but she tells him it isn't necessary — a scant three blocks under the protective glare of streetlamps. He insists, however, and she assents. Will she invite him in? Probably not. The brief stroll is pleasant enough, but it reminds him of unrequited evenings long ago, walking college girls back to their dormitories, when opportunity for romance was already squandered and conversation lost its zest, and the only thing left was a goodnight peck followed by a solitary walk back across the campus.

On the street in front of Teresa's house, he pauses while she continues ahead to the door. "Goodnight," he calls, but she doesn't respond — evidently, her hearing isn't good. She offered no peck, no nothing.

A week later, he phones just to ask how she's doing, and she replies that she is still busy unpacking and assembling her loom. "If you need help, I'm pretty handy with tools," he offers, but she doesn't rise to the bait.

"One of these days I'll have to invite you over," she says, "but things are in too much of a mess right now."

A few days later, he calls again. He has saved the Style section of the Sunday *Post* for her because it's got an article about weaving. He suggests that they meet on the boardwalk at sunset.

I get there first. The sun's almost down. I could be accomplishing more important tasks, like reading e-mail, correcting my manuscript, or making headway in an aging New Yorker, *but I choose to be a nice neighborly guy. A fitting epitaph for me: writer and nice neighborly guy. No, I'm not anticipating my demise anytime soon, but it doesn't hurt to be prepared.*

With ten or twelve others, I watch the sun disappear. Cloudglow in pink and orange and purple. Subdued conversation; I make a point not to catch a word of it (the benches are far enough apart). Intensifying streetlamp aura. The breeze picks up as wavelets turn indigo and lights begin to sparkle along the western shore. Twelve miles distant, the outline of the Bay Bridge becomes a jewel-encrusted swag. I quite forget about Teresa. It's good to be out here this evening — participating in the spectacle but keeping my distance.

Then, peripheral vision cues me to her approach, just around the time mosquitoes ratchet up the nuisance factor. Oh well, I'm good for another five or ten minutes.

Teresa seats herself at the far end of the bench, and I thrust the paper in her direction. Vapidly, she scans the page I've turned down and nods. We exchange few words. Suddenly, she has become the most uninteresting woman in the world to me. She lacks humor, earthiness, inquisitiveness, vitality, mystery, bone structure, and punctuality. We're merely acquaintances — that's all we'll ever be.

Slapping at the insistent insects, Budge rises to his

feet, bids her goodnight, and makes a beeline back to the cottage. He never calls her again and she never calls him.

Chapter 5

A truck is backing up not ten feet from my open window, and the woman in the passenger seat stares right at me. What's going on? I wouldn't mind this invasion of privacy if I had clothes on, but I don't. I'm sitting at my desk quite naked. The morning's already hot, and I just haven't gotten around to getting dressed.

I quickly grasp the situation: the truck's come to pump out the portajohn. Brazenly, I stare back and the woman lowers her gaze (I hope she's not disappointed). At the phragmites border, the truck halts and the driver, a portly fellow in suspenders, climbs down to connect the pumping hose. An odor of disinfectant soon wafts on the breeze. The woman gets out, but she takes a few steps in the opposite direction to look at the bay.

When the emptying's done — it takes no longer than five minutes — the couple remount the cab and come rumbling right past the window again. I haven't moved (I'm busy working). Again the woman looks in, but I'm neither surprised nor offended. I smile at her and she smiles back. Experience has taught me that curiosity thrives on small rewards. Were I in the passenger seat, I'd be doing the same thing. My own curiosity, in fact, may be greater than hers; if I were driving the truck, I'd probably hit the brakes and take a good look. How often does one catch an honest-to-goodness glimpse of a writer in the act — his brow furrowed, his fingers tap-tap-tapping? This lair of a wordsmith is as odd and noteworthy as any in Rock Hall.

48

Budge is finding plenty of solitude — a prerequisite for his work — but with it comes loneliness of a magnitude greater than any he has ever known. His estranged wife isn't having second thoughts and a new lover isn't dropping out of the sky. He doesn't have the inclination or disposable income right now to patronize bars. He is not a churchgoer, he neither golfs nor sails, and he doesn't play bridge. Were it not for the potlucks at the Mainstay and the always dependable sunset club, he'd have no social life to speak of. He has chatted only briefly with his neighbors — as a new single man in their midst, he wants to make sure they understand that he's not a pervert or child molester.

The people next door are elderly, with inflexible daily routines. They go for a stroll around the block at precisely nine o'clock each morning. They call their dog to supper at six. Their mailbox and garbage rituals are as dependable as clockwork. The rest of the time, they spend indoors, doing God-knows-what.

Across the street, the retired economics professor and his wife, a retired audiologist, each take a cup of coffee and a slice of buttered wheat toast to a boardwalk bench by 7:30 a.m., where they sit and importune passersby. Their friendliness constitutes a roadblock to exercise walkers in the vicinity. Budge's own morning routine — a 1.5 mile fast walk — has been waylaid enough times so that he now makes a point of setting forth in the opposite direction.

In fair weather, morning walkers along Beach Road are plentiful and they propel themselves at a good rump-wiggling clip, often in groups of twos and threes. Obese folk and those with dogs, of course, dawdle. Joggers pass by few and far between — a function of the age demographic — although every once in a while a gangly oldster in track shoes comes chuffing along. Whatever the exercise style, a protocol of genteel greeting is unfailingly adhered to: on a typical circuit, Budge will call out "Good Morning!" as many as twenty or thirty times.

Every "good morning" is a reaffirmation that I'm not entirely alone, although such slight and impersonal contact, over and over, isn't conducive to a real feeling of connectedness. I picture myself bidding "good morning" to strangers for the rest of my life — not a particularly sanguine glimpse of the future, but if this is the best I can do, I'll have to live with it. Starting off the day in this fashion makes me at least thankful to be ambulatory.

On his walks, Budge never fails to notice the women, although the single ones are usually not up to snuff and the good-looking ones always have partners — businessmen, yachtsmen, whatever. Taking stock of the various female physiques and physiognomies, he will sometimes experience a razor pang of regret for losing his wife, although he is careful not to allow himself to get carried away again and start talking to her, i.e., talking to himself. He is gaining more control, especially in public; he doesn't want to be branded a babbling idiot. He finds, moreover, that when he puts a lid on self-conversation, his thoughts tend not to dwell in the past.

Every footstep is an increment toward healing, he reminds himself. Getting out is synonymous with getting over. But *looking* outward is the real key, and that can also be done from within the confines of the cottage.

I've grown to relish this proximity to strangers. They provide me with a yardstick to measure my own insularity by. Take, for instance, the young woman and her child under the locust tree just outside my window. It's a hot afternoon; clad only in underwear, I'm toiling at my desk with the electric fan on. The woman has spread a blanket in the shade and is lying on her back fast asleep — not 25 feet away from me! — while the child sits in a folding chair, absorbed in a picture book. I find myself studying the woman's features: short and spiky bleach-blonde hair, angular cheekbones, sculpted lips snoozingly parted. Beneath the fabric of her T-shirt, her breasts jut to either side, obedient to both brassiere and gravity. Her hands are folded across her stomach, and her legs, emerging from shorts, are twin tapering logs bumped at the kneecap. She could be an artist's model, a perfectly still specimen for transliteration to another medium. I want to sketch her. The angle of her bare feet reminds me of Manet's dying toreador.

But I'm afraid that the slightest commotion on my part might break the spell. Instead, I just sit there and watch. So oblivious to the world is she that it becomes contagious. After ten minutes or so, I'm inspired to shut down the computer and go into the bedroom for a nap.

The heat of August slows everything down except tourism. Along Beach Road, every place is rented, with SUVs hunkering in the driveways. Rainbow-colored pennants are fastened to porch posts and flagpoles, signifying residency. The beach draws sunbathers and onlookers and a few intrepid swimmers (the stinging jellyfish are at their peak). Youngsters wade and splash, skip stones, excavate oyster shells, explore the reedy promontory beyond the portajohn. On a sweltering Saturday afternoon, almost every square foot of sand is accounted for by either a blanket or a body or a cooler.

You might even say it resembles Coney Island — on a

51

much reduced scale. It makes me wonder why all these people have congregated here, when an ocean beach is less than two hours distant. That's where the real action is: miles of sand and surf, boardwalk amenities, midway thrills, high-rises. Who'd settle for Rock Hall when they could have Ocean City?

But I answer my own question. Maybe they're here for the same reason I am. There's no substitute for a friendly small town atmosphere. You can be unfashionable, you can be out of step. You can disobey the "Beach Rules" sign and nobody, not even the local constabulary, gives a hoot. Stores and restaurants are ten short blocks away; you can hop on the trolley and be there in minutes. And most important of all, Chesapeake Bay holds a quieter allure. You watch the sun go down across the water without neon stabbing you in the back.

Budge doesn't mean to sound like a civic booster, but his attitude is changing. He's growing comfortable in his newfound home. He's not so on edge. If anything, he's come to terms with his loneliness, realizing that it may take months to alleviate. Meanwhile, he's determined to make the best of it, although the heat keeps him indoors during the daytime and he rarely deviates from his writing schedule.

In the early evenings he'll sometimes take a drive in the old Corolla just to cool off and clear his brain.

Getting away from the cottage, however briefly, becomes a mental necessity. I don't go far — over to Tolchester where the shipping channel cuts near the shoreline, or down to the wildlife sanctuary on Eastern Neck Island. Sometimes I just drive around Rock Hall itself — Catholic Avenue, Boundary Avenue, Liberty

Street, Hawthorne Avenue, Sharp Street. Dead-ends and alleyways, water accesses, cul-de-sacs.

Yes, I know. Mindless cruising is a silly holdover, a figment of my long-gone youth, a waste of gasoline. Having no real destination or purpose, I'm the worst kind of automotive polluter — the guy who buys a tankful and proceeds to burn it for no good reason. Motion for motion's sake, an idiotic expenditure of energy!

I only wish I had a woman to ride shotgun.

There are other diversions as well. On a mid-August Saturday, Rock Hall's annual "Party on the Bay," is held at the town bulkhead, a harborside expanse between wharves and boat sheds not far from where he lives. The day is a scorcher and he normally eschews both crowds and midday sun, but this is an event he feels he shouldn't miss. He has already devoted the morning to writing and just now had lunch.

Sometimes it's good to do what everyone else is doing. All morning I've looked out the window and seen cars heading in that direction. I'm ready to join the procession so off I saunter with maximum protection — canvas hat, long trousers and sleeves, sunblock. Along the half-mile hike, I'm stopped twice and asked directions, which makes me feel like a true Rock Haller.

Budge arrives at the bulkhead to find the party in full swing. Several hundred people are milling between two rows of shade canopies flanking a bandstand and a covered picnic area. The three-piece band is rhythmically obstreperous — guitarist, bassist, singing drummer — as a contingent of mostly women sidesteps in unison to the slide boogie. A beer seller ministers to his parched gregarious queue. Adjacent food purveyors dispense funnel cakes, pit beef sandwiches, Philly steaks, steamed shrimp, Italian sausage, and caramel apple chips. When the band takes a break, a crab-picking contest ensues. From the crowd, bashful half-drunk souls are importuned, seated at a table, given three minutes to extract the meat of whole crabs into pint containers. The winner — by weight — is awarded twenty-five dollars.

Off in the harbor, pleasure craft peopled to the gunwales ride at anchor. The skipjack *Nathan* nudges pierside between half-hour cruises — not cheap, never crowded. By contrast, the free shuttle boat to Waterman's Dock on the far side of the harbor is jammed. In the glare of the afternoon, Budge is thankful for his ray-deflecting attire, although he can't help but notice that most of the partygoers, young and old, celebrate the sun. Hatless, with minimal covering, tanned in some cases to precancerous (so he imagines) excess, they circulate in multitude, flaunting body piercings and tattoos.

Centrally located in the throng is Rock Hall's Oysterman, a life-size bronze heroic figure on a pedestal, frozen forever in the act of harvest. Within his long-handled tongs' basket, someone has placed real oyster shells, an elegiac reminder of a once-thriving Chesapeake Bay industry, now diminished almost to the point of extinction.

The crowd ignores the statue. It isn't pirouetting, it isn't hawking anything, it isn't decked out in polychrome, and it has been around for years. Its patina looks almost black. An African-American oysterman? All the more reason to ignore it.

By three o'clock in the afternoon, with the heat at its oppressive zenith, business under the shade canopies begins to slack off. Handmade hats, ornamental birdhouses, toe rings, Nautical Treasures, sports plaques, plastic bag holders, and other assorted "bayside" crafts go unsold. Out by the parking lot, fewer children jump and slide and squeal in the inflatable fun-house. J.R.'s Midnight Express, back on the bandstand, belts out another set, but nobody's dancing anymore despite the fact that the country-rockers have cranked the volume.

On the crowd's outskirts, I stand in the slim shade of a utility pole to listen awhile to the music, although by now my ears don't perceive it as such. Nor do I get relief from the heat; the pavement broils through the soles of my sneakers. I have no choice but to keep moving.

Circumnavigating the bulkhead one last time, he exchanges greetings with two or three familiar faces and picks up a few free pencils and refrigerator magnets. Then he walks home.

Chapter 6

As August wears on, Budge stays on the premises for even longer stretches. He's making a concerted effort to spend less money — not by choice, but by necessity. Having balanced his checkbook, he realizes that unless he can generate more income, he will be broke within two billing cycles.

In a way, it's a good thing that he's *not* dating anyone — he can't afford to. But why is he staying at home day and night, not availing himself of even so minor a perk as an occasional ice cream sundae at Durdings or Saturday night concert at the Mainstay? He is putting himself at an extreme social and personal disadvantage, and for what? Is he trying to prove to himself that he can scrimp like a pauper?

No, it's to prove to the world that he's a serious writer, a literary force to be reckoned with despite his obscurity and advancing years.

I sit at my desk and write. That's all I do, day in and day out. I intend to write my way out of this predicament, write my way to a pedestal of modest renown. I know I can do it — writing is the one thing I do better than anything else. Somewhere, somehow, someone will want to read these words. In my lifetime, I hope.

I used to consider myself the most versatile writer in the world. Give me any topic, and I'd custom craft a piece of required length. I was an indefatigable researcher; I got right down to the nitty-gritty. I thought of my skills as being superior to those of a mere reporter, because I pol-

ished my prose to a high literary lustre — I didn't just serve it up hardboiled.

One by one, these projects were completed, but then freelance work became scarce. Nowadays, choice writing assignments are doled out in-house — staff writers are easier to control and paid less. A new generation of editors, having little affinity for a writing style like mine, applies the red pencil too heavily. My sentences are diced into a succotash of mediocrity, and what I see in print isn't at all what I've submitted.

Budge is on a favorite topic here: the hard truth about growing obsolete.

But you don't stop doing what you do best. If you do, you're fooling yourself. Recently, there has been a lot of talk about "reinventing," i.e., dropping one persona and picking up another as easily as, say, slipping on a Halloween mask. The ultimate versatility: turning into a new and different person (and tossing in a little cosmetic surgery, if it'll help to complete the transformation). Then what do you have? A creature desperate for approval. A man or woman who will do anything to obfuscate the old reality. Learn new skills, wear new clothes, drive a new car, take a new lover. But in the end, you're left with a makeover that will fail as surely as what was in place to begin with. Life is short; its potential is limited; its possibilities are finite. This is what's known, I think, as "the human condition."

When the writing day is over, Budge finds solace in quaffing a beer or two at the water's edge. Starting roughly at the portajohn, there is a low wall of rip-rap extending through the phragmites, and on these piled up rocks, completely hidden from the public beach, Budge has placed an Adirondack chair that washed up shortly after he first moved in. As found objects go, the chair is a rarity; it must have cost a couple of hundred dollars when new. Its teak slats, fastened with stainless steel screws, are in near-perfect condition — nicely weathered, too — with only one armrest cracked. Budge toiled for almost an hour one afternoon to get the chair situated atop the massive granite polyhedrons so that its four legs were level and sufficiently wedged against the highest tides. Now he has a veritable throne on the bay.

This is where I go as the day draws to a close. Later, I'll mosey over to the boardwalk to visit with whoever is representing the sunset club that evening, but first I want to relax by myself and not worry about getting busted for having an open container of alcohol.

Ragu accompanies me. After checking the rustling vegetation for scents and quarry, she stretches out upon one of the flatter rocks below the chair. She has no interest in the bay splendor, while I can't take my eyes off it. As the sun lowers, the water turns successive shades of chiaroscuro, and the reflective movement over so vast an area, linked to the sky by a sliver of distant shoreline, is nothing short of mind-bending. It's easy to lose all track of time.

Condensation from the beer bottle runs down the arm of the chair. Mosquitoes violate my airspace. I shift my posterior to a more comfortable position. My feet are swinging free (the chair sits high, it couldn't be helped). Several small craft are in view: a charter fishing boat returning to the harbor, two sailboats tilted in the evening breeze, a speedboat copping a last rush of adrenaline. Through binoculars, I can make out tractor trailers rolling along the highway on Kent Island — darkly shimmering rectangles slowly traversing the horizon. A couple of feet in front and below my chair, opaque brown wavelets rush and recede, rush and recede, tumbling a dead fish that aromatically wedges itself between rocks.

I am that breeze, I am those trucks, I am that dead fish! I'm here because I want to be here — no, that's not it at all. I don't want to be here; I have to be here, and there's nothing I can do about it. I am one with this shoreline, wedded to it, stuck with it. For how long, I have no idea. Christ, it's a bummer!

In the hottest part of the day, when Budge is indoors, he uses the binoculars for closer subjects.

I hardly consider myself a Peeping Tom — I mean, voyeuristically speaking, the bathing beauties are in plain view — but this way, I can extend my appreciation of bare flesh to details I might otherwise miss. A sprinkle of freckles, a felicitously placed mole, a birthmark the antonym of a blemish, a pierced navel, a tasteful tattoo, a noteworthy manicure or pedicure, a ravishing sunburn, a clump of bleached still-wet hair. What better way for a non-sunworshipper to study the noonday colonization of the strand? Optical enhancement brings me close-up without getting personal. I'm paying the rent, I'm entitled to the view.

Thoreau said something about how the unexamined life is not worth living. I couldn't agree more. My powers of observation are my true wealth (not to mention my sole source of entertainment). My eyes lead me to contemplations that are key to my well-being. Were I to ignore the minutiae, I'd be all the poorer. Myopic as the next guy, I'd miss a good portion of what "beachness" is, too.

It is a privilege to live here, I keep reminding myself.

*This is no recirculating frog pond, no whooshing white
noise machine that plugs into an outlet beside the bed.
This is the "real deal" — and on Beach Road no less! It
looks and smells and sounds just right. It's got a human
component that invites scrutiny. But I don't just think of
myself as an observer of female anatomy; I also observe
context, proportion, quality, and relationship. Hence I
have no qualms about using the tools at my disposal.*

Thus Budge rationalizes his surreptitious surveillance
without mentioning his actual motivation, i.e., the sheer
horniness that compounds daily. Were it not for the binoculars, he'd have no outlet — however vicarious — for his
pent-up tactile urges. From inside the cottage, however, he
lacks an unimpeded view. Double panes of dirty glass plus
screening dull the clarity, and the locust trees and boxwood — not to mention the two kiosks — partially block
the sight line. So he doesn't get to see everything he might
want to (of course, if he stepped outside, that would solve
the problem).

But Budge isn't an in-your-face guy, nor does he want
the reputation of a dirty old man. He's too busy, he's got
too much work to do. He'll only glance up from the computer screen every fifteen minutes or so. For a writer as
unsuccessful as he has been lately, he still retains an amazing amount of discipline. He continues to believe in the
Big Payoff. He'll gawk through the binoculars only to rest
his eyes. A full day's writing always comes first.

This may explain why, during off hours, his imagination often runs out of control. Take, for example, the simple act of grocery shopping at Bayside Foods. Like most
men, Budge would rather not shop, but since he has to, he
utilizes the opportunity to give the once-over to two
checkout girls in particular.

Both are in their late teens, both physically stunning. One is tall with ash blond tresses, the other is petite with a dirty blond bouffant. The ash-blonde has a vacuity that takes my breath away; her eyes stare through me as if I'm not there. She's got thin lips, a beak of a nose, a complexion of the palest ivory. Checking the groceries, she hunches forward and squints a little — not out of concentration, but out of boredom — as she shoves each item lackadaisically across the scanner. Something in her attitude turns me on — her passivity, her disdain. She's a fully clothed paper doll waiting for a lover.

The other, the dirty-blonde, is just the opposite. She's cute, talkative, eager to please. When greeting customers, she looks directly into their eyes and smirks coquettishly. She's got the most kissible lips in creation (I often wonder who they're being wasted on). The acne on her rosy cheeks has almost disappeared (from sunbathing at the beach?), and her lithe post-adolescent figure — from what I can see of it — is in exquisite proportion. She makes me feel like I'm her valued customer (could she secretly have the hots for me?). Moving my purchases over the laser window, taking my cash and proffering the receipt, her multi-ringed hands articulate the age-old transaction between seller and buyer. Her bagging skills are superior to anybody's in the store. She's so helpful, in fact, that after she loads each plastic sack, she stiffens the handles by creasing them so they're upright and ready for the grabbing. I only wish it were as easy to grab her...

Okay, enough of that. A steady diet of Budge's romanticization of the mundane can choke the swallower. What kind of an audience is he writing for, anyway? More and more, it appears he's writing only for himself. No wonder he's having a hard time getting published! It's easy for him to get carried away on descriptive flights of fancy, just as it's easy for him to forget his age and the way he really appears in a mirror.

On the other hand, Budge is a sane man. Which means, of course, that he's perfectly harmless. He's a mainstream guy with mainstream values; it wouldn't dawn on him in a million years to actually make a pass at a teenage girl. (If he ever did, God forbid, he wouldn't know what to do next.) At present, the only thing that distinguishes him from any other average middle-aged Joe is that he is very, very lonely and he's got an overstimulated imagination. He is a dumped writer — those two words say it all. Can he not be blamed, then, for being woman-hungry man incarnate? He's got one thing on his mind and, rant as he might, it seems to be the farthest thing from his grasp.

Similarly, when Budge goes to the post office on Liberty Street, he is smitten.

Rosa, behind the counter, is the most beautiful woman in Rock Hall. I'm talking about ripeness now, not teeny-bopper immaturity. Rosa's beauty radiates beyond the depredations of time; she's like a Florentine matron, knowledgeable yet demure, with a face that would rival Helen's, launcher of a thousand ships. She's in her mid-50s (it takes one to know one), with colored hair, wrinkled brow, a sagging jawline (you can tell if she's having a good day or a bad one) and penetrating dark eyes. She's got fleshy arms and is at least ten pounds overweight with a bit of a tummy (fibroids?), but she's an out-and-out delight to gaze upon.

When I walk in, she is usually at the back of the office, sorting behind the one-way glass. "I'll be there in just a minute," she'll call in that sultry voice which utterly cap-

tivates me. I imagine her stepping nude from behind an ornate screen, an Odalisque summoned by her lover. I brace myself for the treat. When she does appear, crisp and business-like in her postal attire, I do my best not to make the transaction too brief. "Oh, and I need some stamps, too. Do you have any new issues? Would you mind showing me?"

She always obliges. My eyes flit between the stamps and her. Without a doubt, she has a face that launches thousands of pieces of priority mail. Do others see her beauty as well? Does her husband (deduced by the wedding band) worship her as I do? He'd be a curmudgeon if he didn't. In my estimation, Rosa is the town's single most valuable asset. In her presence I grow weak-kneed and light-headed — she has that strong an effect upon me. Naturally, I hold myself together, but I buy more stamps than I need.

Thus, the pattern emerges. Budge can't help himself, roving from one feminine superlative to the next. He's a lover's lover, with no means of expressing himself other than in prose that curls purple at the edges with unrequited desire. The strain of this state of suspended sexuality will surely drive him nuts.

Chapter 7

Budge describes his loneliness to a doctor in Chestertown during a routine checkup. Physically, he's feeling fine, except for the fact that he's not sleeping very well. Dr. Schneider commends him on his weight, blood pressure, and blood work — obtained just recently — as well as his general state of fitness. The stethoscope plus pokings and proddings and orifice-inspecting confirm the diagnosis: here sits a strikingly healthy 55-year-old male.

Without saying so, Budge is greatly relieved.

"As for sleeping pills," the physician advises, "I'd prefer not to write you a prescription. Try to relax a little more — drink a glass or two of wine every night, watch a good movie, read a book, and when you're ready, start dating again..."

Budge interrupts. "That's the problem, Doc. I'm definitely ready — believe me, I'm rarin' to go — but I can't find a suitable woman."

Budge then goes on to inquire if there's a local support group for divorced people. Considering the question, Dr. Schneider strokes his chin thoughtfully.

"A local support group, you say? Right off, I can't think of any. We're too far from a metropolitan area. But I'll tell you what — you go online, don't you?"

Budge acknowledges that he does.

"Look up a singles website — there are hundreds of 'em. Give it a shot. Good luck!"

Budge drives back to Rock Hall in a mood of rare elation.

Never was there a simpler or more elegant solution to friendlessness! Why didn't I think of it before? A few keystrokes, and I can hand-pick the partner of my dreams. What could be easier? Message to all the lonely women in North America: I'll soon have you in my crosshairs and one of you is gonna get lucky — maybe tonight!

When the writing day is done, he fires up the search engine and starts clicking through the websites. Women are everywhere, brilliantly bracketed between pop-up ads. On first glance, the postage-stamp-size cameos nearly overwhelm him with their variety. Scrolling with a novice's inquisitiveness, Budge evaluates them at his leisure like a pasha inspecting his harem. Yes, no, no, no, yes, no, maybe. One after another, the tiny lipsticked smiles glint back at him. Never before have so many women vied for his attention. The relational reaching out across this great land is far more widespread than he would have imagined. He's strongly tempted to insert his own image in this human meat market stretching from the Atlantic to the Pacific, up into Canada and down into Mexico.

It makes him reflect, too, on the myriad ways relationships end and single lives begin. Each cameo is a story — likely as not, a painful one — that continues to supply confusion, resentment, and depression in large inchoate doses despite the glinting smile.

Upon closer inspection, certain patterns demarcate the decades. Women in their 30s look best — trim, lank-haired, easy on his defect meter. In their 40s, they're wearing loosely fitted blouses and their hairdos have become artful helmets. Sexiness is no longer inherent, but packaged as a commodity (*come and get it, I've still got it*). In their 50s, they're permed-up grandmas hiding themselves in muumuus or flaunting their figures in décolleté party clothes — either way, they look unappetizing.

Budge is taken aback.

These gals are my age. These are the ones — seasoned veterans of life's vicissitudes — I should identify with the most, yet I pass by their pictures as quickly as possible. Heaven forbid I should wind up with one of these creatures! Nevertheless, guilt suffuses me. I feel as if I should castigate myself, but on what grounds? Because their physical appeal is lacking? If a female contemporary said that of me, I'd take great offense. Because they've got a used-up look? I look at myself in the mirror and think exactly the same thing. Because they're doing the best they can with what they've got, and it's not good enough? I'm a prime example of a has-been who won't give up.

In rejecting them, I'm rejecting myself, and it makes me feel like a shit. A worthless fraudulent fooling-nobody-but-himself shit. Our society's youth culture clutches me — and you too, dear reader — by the balls. I want a tight-assed high-breasted chick (I don't want a dowdy brood hen). I can't function unless I think of myself as young. Consumer products and services have drugged me to the point that, without them, I'd wander around in circles, aimlessly searching for validation. We all need wooden daggers thrust into our vampire hearts to put us out of our materialistic misery.

A cogent enough rant, but does Budge practice what he preaches? No, not at all. In a man like him, ageism and sexism can't be extirpated overnight. Despite what his moralistic brain propounds, his discriminating eye holds sway. He is looking for a femme fatale who'll knock his socks off.

66

So there he sits, poring over the numerous offerings in the aforementioned age brackets (wisely, he passes up the twenty-somethings, but only because he fears becoming a laughingstock). He reads a sample biographical sketch or two; he is particularly titillated by the "I'll tell you later" entries for weight, income, favorite TV shows, desire for children. Even going this far, Budge is picky. If she smokes, he's not interested. If she's the slightest bit pious, ditto. If she likes pets, that's fine, but if she's a Chihuahua fancier, forget it. He is gratified to see that so many women like to dance (could this have been a factor in breakups — the uptight hubby who refused to twirl his missus 'round the floor, even on anniversaries?).

Most of the women classify themselves as light-to-moderate social drinkers. Most list "long walks in the rain" and "listening to opera" among their favorite activities, followed by watching sunsets (he can relate to that!). There is frequent mention of sharing "quiet intimate moments," or simply "dinner by candlelight." A surprising number of women are interested in men younger than themselves. About half have no objection to dating outside their race.

He clicks further to read in-depth self-advertisements, sections variously titled, "Who I Really Am," "What Turns Me On," and "What I'm Looking For In A Man," but the webserver automatically cuts him off. He's had his free introduction, now he's got to pony up. Only by typing in I.D. and address info, plus those all-important credit card numbers, will he be allowed to proceed through the electronic portal. Membership is only $9.95 a month, with unlimited access to chat rooms and private e-mail with hundreds of gorgeous available women. The computer will instantly match him to female club-members who share similar interests and expectations — within whichever mile radius he chooses. He can search close to home or across the entire continent. Insistent, throbbing icons urge him to start typing. Once he is a member, he won't regret it. Loneliness will be a thing of the past.

But Budge hesitates. The invisible wall of his anonymity holds him back. He also knows that he can ill afford the additional monthly expense. Moreover, the women undergo a subtle transformation when he clicks to enlarge their images. Every face appears slightly desperate. This in itself isn't a negative attribute – he is desperate, too — but credit card debt is hard to justify under the circumstances.

Scrolling down the search engine links, he finds another website that shows more promise — "Free Basic Membership With No Obligation!" It's a Canadian singles club featuring comely women and a less hyper format. Heartened, Budge clicks to enter. This won't cost him anything, so it's worth a try. To hell with anonymity!

Without hesitation now, he fills the boxes with relevant data. A nickname is required; after giving it some thought, he types *BetweenBooks*. He congratulates himself for setting the perfect tone — it shows that he is an established intellectual, a serious-minded individual, and it also implies, with panache (so he thinks), that he is finished with one relationship and ready to start another. Oh, he's clever at double entendre! This will put him in contact with a real highbrow, somebody of his caliber, a woman who reads books — possibly even writes them! — and can hold an intelligent conversation. Maybe a Ph.D., maybe a University of Toronto professor of English Lit. who lives in a high-rise overlooking Lake Ontario. A willowy brunette with glasses, someone on the order of Victoria Sinclair of *Naked News*. In his mind's eye, he sees himself occupying the high-rise with her, acclimatizing to the cold weather and taking up winter sports. A stint in Canada would broaden his heretofore limited horizon. It could lead to bi-lingualism, dual citizenship, an expanded market for his books.

Enthusiastically, he checks off the appropriate boxes. He, too, is a light-to-moderate drinker. He is nonreligious, has one pet, likes children (and leaves open the possibility of having them), doesn't do drugs, and is willing to move anywhere to start a new life. He will reveal his estimated salary later. He is not sure whether to say he is bald or has gray hair – he is a combination of both but can check only one — so he admits to the latter.

Then comes the creative part, the anticipation of which causes Budge to smack his lips. "Please Describe Yourself in 300 Words or Less."

He will shine at this; fifty-five years of self-knowledge should provide plenty of input.

I'm a guy who lives life in large draughts. I enjoy almost everything, as much as I can get. I love people, good times, food & drink (candlelit dinners a specialty), movies, classical music (including opera), baseball, politics, travel, history, big cities, small towns, and the great outdoors (esp. long walks in the rain). I love curling up before a fireplace with a good book (if I've got someone to curl up with, that's even better). I keep abreast of current events. I have a hearty sense of humor. I'm honest, nonjudgmental, patient, caring, and forgiving. I don't play the blame game and I don't hold grudges. I make friends easily and am a trusted confidant.

An author by profession, I'm an acute observer of what goes on around me as well as an experienced partaker, so I consider myself something of an expert in this one-way self-aware journey through time that we call life.

This also means that I'm a good listener. I deal with situations as they arise and make the best of them. I've had my share of troubles — who hasn't? — but I've always approached their solution with optimism and have, by and large, succeeded. I'm a stickler for good health and clean living; I don't believe in hobbling myself with bad habits. I look only on the bright side.

I believe in a Supreme Being, miracles, angels, the Toronto Bluejays, motherhood & apple pie, the coming of universal peace & prosperity, and the infinite resourcefulness of the human spirit. I believe the power of love is transcendent, and that the human touch is the most healing quantum we know and will ever know. I believe that a soul-mate is out there waiting for me, and when we make the connection, her personal sphere will overflow with gratification and fulfillment. She will be enveloped in respect and tenderness and affection, and I solemnly promise — even before we meet — that I will never let her down. If you happen to be reading this and think you are she, please get in touch. Otherwise, I will find you. Don't be discouraged.

Have I exceeded 300 words? Well, it shows that my personality doesn't fit narrow confines. I'm a lover plenipotentiary, a millennial Byron, a student of the wide romantic world. I may be the only one left, so don't delay in your response!

In the onscreen box provided, Budge reviews and refines his sentiments. Some classy babe will bite, he tells himself. This is no minor league con job. The time and effort he is putting into this project ought to snag a "ten" for sure.

Similarly, he tackles the second 300-word essay, "What I'm Looking For in a Woman."

The woman I seek must be true to herself, not a composite of other peoples' expectations. If you're neurotic and dependent on approval, or if you lie about your age and lack the basic confidence to give 100% of yourself in a secure relationship, read no further.

Having addressed these negatives — I'm sorry they had to come out first, but I got burned in an LTR recently by someone who exhibited all these traits (yes, I should've known better) — let me concentrate on the positives. You're trim, educated, orgasmic, witty, faithful, forgiving, a fashionable dresser, a reader (editing skills a plus), a good writer, a good sport, a birdwatcher (novice status okay), a willing dance-partner, and a decent cook (that's the skill level I claim, and that's good enough). You're easygoing around animals, you're not freaked by spiders, bats, or snakes. You're helpful around the house because you understand that a woman's home is her castle, too. You're not stuck on yourself, but you exude a sense of pride. You don't object categorically to a man's point of view, which you know is bound to be different from your own.

You see the man in your life as a complement to you, not a tolerated adversary. You don't exclude him from activities you enjoy. You try to take pleasure in the same things he does, but if for some reason you can't, then you don't hold it against him. You like sex, but what's more, you understand how important it is for a man, and so you encourage him both as a lover and an object to be loved. You don't hold yourself back.

You are inventive, energetic, self-motivated, flexible, and willing to cope with the lows as well as the highs. You, too, want a soul-mate, not just an arm trophy.

If you can truthfully, joyously admit that all the above applies to you, then what are you waiting for? Let's find each other and share the rapture — forever, if it works out.

Well, that ought to do the trick. He has made himself irresistible. "I can expect a full inbox tonight," he gloats aloud.

He scrolls back through the application, making sure he answered everything. Oops, he forgot to give the age bracket for the women he's seeking. He punches 30 to 39, but has immediate misgivings; it looks superficial, coming from a man of his years. He corrects the numbers: 39 to 55. Yes, that's better, it makes him look like a real connoisseur. This way, he is neither robbing the cradle nor desecrating the grave.

Satisfied, he goes back to the bottom of the text and clicks the enter button. "Welcome home, BetweenBooks," the next screen blares, listing the basic membership options he can avail himself of right away to get started on his quest for companionship. For openers, he can post a picture of himself and check his website mailbox for messages. Presumably, the main-frame has already matched him to likely candidates. Suddenly, a full-screen advertisement pops down: "Apply For Premium Membership Now! Only $9.95 Per Month Including Our Free Newsletter!"

It turns out that basic membership offers little, if anything. He can look at the same tiny portraits he has already seen. He can read the women's thumbnail bios, but nothing more detailed. He can receive e-mail, but he can't send it. He can amend his application (but why bother?).

Premium membership, on the other hand, really gets the ball rolling. There's online chat, direct emailing, geographical searching and winnowing, full access to personal essays (like what he just labored over), plus exciting games and full-screen photos.

But his pecuniary situation can't be ignored. For the

moment, he has to forego premium membership. His finely wrought expository prose has been in vain!

Dismayed, Budge closes the window. So much for the online freebie. Over the next two weeks, he logs on a few times, hoping that he has been discovered, but there is nothing more than the chummy, "Welcome home, BetweenBooks!" and an empty inbox save for the initial message congratulating him for signing up. Like a guillotine, the premium membership ad descends, and he is cut off once again.

The day soon arrives when he is fed up with the whole computer match-up business. It's just another scam; he should have known better. Loneliness has left him vulnerable, and now his privacy — online *and* in real life — may be imperiled. Moreover, he's ashamed to have written the things he did. How dare he quantify himself — or worse, an imaginary woman — for all the world to see? Where is his natural reserve, his dignity? Those highfalutin sentiments revealed his own insecurities and ignorance. What does he really know about who he is or what he wants?

He logs on, repulsed by the bursting salutation that now offends him with its hyper-familiarity. What impudence! — to be welcomed by a machine. This isn't his home, not by a longshot. And what in the world made him give himself such an idiotic nickname? But wait! There is a new message.

"Hi BetweenBook my name is Tiffani you sound like you are ok we might hit it off you never know I am fun."

Budge looks out to the water and shakes his head sadly.

Tiffani, wherever you are, please understand that it's nothing personal. I'm not answering because I know with 99.99% certitude that you and I have absolutely nothing in common, nothing to build on. You wrote a brave inquiry, and I wish you luck. Please accept my silence and do not bother to write again.

Well, at least he examined the ethereal avenue — Thoreau would approve. But he'd better backspace out of the club right away lest he be suckered, in a weak moment, into a membership upgrade. Who knows what danger is lurking — viruses electronic and venereal, stolen identity, a deluge of spam, cookies, worms...

Budge clicks on the "Admin." button and locates the delete prompts. He then sets about obliterating every box he filled in, including the two that took him at least an hour apiece.

"We're sorry to see you leave, BetweenBooks," the next screen reads. "Reason for terminating membership?"

"Found someone," he types.

Chapter 8

It can be inferred, then, that Budge badly needs to get out of town. He has made no discernible progress with the local available women and he is no longer tempted to seek romance over the Internet. Working day after day on his roman à clef is beginning to drag him down. His compulsive writing habit is robbing him of leisure time. The beach activity and bay view aren't holding his interest like they used to. Even the incessant presence of the ospreys aggravates him.

I'm belatedly realizing that ospreys are stupid birds, perhaps the stupidest around. Their peep-peeping has got to be nature's most idiotic vocalization, and once they're started, they can't stop. They just perch on a snag or piling and peep their pea-brains out — it's not a mating call or a call to dinner or a communication of any kind. It's a "here I am" affirmation, lasting for minutes on end, and it drives me bonkers.

Ospreys look stupid, too — they're pinheads. Small-beaked, with white and brown stripes, heads poke above their large brown bodies like misshapen periscopes. Also ridiculous-looking are the talons, oversize scimitars that resemble those of certain ladies competing for fingernail length in the Guinness Book of Records.

Okay, the big birds soar elegantly enough — what avian of prey doesn't? — but they regularly drop the fish they snatch. An osprey's clumsiness manifests itself in other ways, too. The other day I watched one trying to land in a dead tree at the edge of the backyard, and it took three swooping tries to get vector and airspeed right. The bird had chosen the tip of a near-vertical branch to alight upon — a lousy choice for a landing zone — necessitating two awkward bailouts. Finally, the osprey came in just right; its talons clutched the branch and with a great clumsy flapping, it gained balance. It then proceeded to eject a whopping white spatter, narrowly missing me.

Nature's entertainment value aside, Budge is running out of steam. Along with his writing notes, his desk is cluttered with reminders of things left undone — queries to submit, bills to pay, quarterly tax forms to fill out. He desperately needs a change of scene, if only for a day.

Fortunately, he just sold another short piece, entitled "An Insider's Rock Hall," to a biweekly publication mostly filled with ads. The pay isn't great, but it promises to lead to other assignments. He is worried, though, that if readers knew how short a time he has lived here, they might question his expertise. At any rate, for the first time in weeks, he's got a little spending money.

Coincidentally, he has received an invitation to a recital at the Curtis Institute in Philadelphia. The daughter of an old college pal is giving a performance as part of her degree requirement in voice. How Budge got on her mailing list, he doesn't know, but he hastily accepts this perfect excuse for a getaway. The invitation also mentions that family and friends will be getting together at a restaurant for a late supper after the recital. He looks forward to joining them.

On the appointed day, then, he aims the trusty Corolla away from Rock Hall.

How exhilarating it is to be leaving this place! A big city fix — hallelujah! Eagerly, I drive toward the four-lan-

ers — Routes 301 and 896, then I-95. The more traffic, the merrier! Exhaust fumes, numbing blankness of corporate scenery — no problem! Aggressive drivers, tailgaters, rubberneckers, bottlenecks, construction delays — no problem! After two hours on the road, the spires of Philadelphia welcome me like beckoning saints. Hey Ben, whassup? I work my way toward Locust Street and Rittenhouse Square, luck out with parking, greet these folks I haven't seen in years.

In the recital hall, the proud father and his entourage are seated early, allowing plenty of time for gabbing and catching up. Budge's old pal accepts his singlehood with nary a raised eyebrow, causing him to wonder if the fellow knew all along that his marriage wouldn't last.

Do people from your past understand you better, because they've seen what makes you tick long before your chickens came home to roost, so to speak? It's a plausible theory.

The house lights dim and the accompanist walks onstage, taking a bow and seating herself at the nine-foot grand piano. She is a tiny, intense young woman in a black pantsuit with long curly black hair that shines in the spotlight. Then the vocalist enters, bowing thrice to the swelling applause.

Wow! The years have turned the skanky teenager I remember into a strapping young soprano. Exquisitely coiffured and gowned, she exudes the stage presence of a pro. As the first chords are struck, she lilts into a program of 19th-century German leider. I'm immediately impressed by her dynamism and range...

It's a long recital, note perfect insofar as his ears can tell and received with a standing ovation. Cameras flash, there is an encore, bouquets are proffered. After the applause dies away, Budge approaches the stage with the others to give his personal congratulations, but the young soprano is quite surrounded by well-wishers. Alternately, he walks over to the accompanist and introduces himself.

Her name is Nadia Valarian and she's got the most intelligent eyes I've ever looked into — black pools of sheer brainpower, that's what they are. Close up, she's even more diminutive than from a distance — just a slip of a youngster, a tightly wound coil of pianistic energy with old-world manners and English-as-a-second-language charm. I tell her she did an outstanding job (in truth, I often found myself listening closer to her than to the vocalist). Flattered by my words — and perhaps grateful for my attention — she's responsive and friendly.

Since nobody else is monopolizing her at the moment, Budge has Nadia all to himself, and he wastes no time peppering her with questions and more compliments. It turns out, she is from Kyrgyzstan; her family immigrated here five years ago. Her mother is a violinist and her father is a composer. She started piano lessons in Toshkent, Kyrgyzstan's capital city, when she was four years old.

Under the sponsorship of relatives in Philadelphia, the family gradually adapted to the crazy quilt culture of the United States — she smiles knowingly as she recounts this. Her musical education and performance schedule are continuing uninterrupted. Her mother now has steady work in pit orchestras and her father is beginning to get film scores. She has a younger sister, too, who is gifted on the clarinet.

It dawns on me that I'm conversing with a child prodigy. When I ask where she has performed, she mentions cities like St. Petersburg, Vienna, Berlin, Helsinki. Two years ago she gave a concert in New York City — Carnegie Hall, as a matter of fact.
My line of questioning turns oafish. Quickly, I've gone beyond my depth, struggling to sound knowledgeable, but mainly flabbergasted in the presence of musical genius. She fields my queries with amused interest. I can't help becoming deferential. She is the unheralded star of the evening; she's the one who should be receiving the bouquets.

Later, at the restaurant, Budge excuses himself from his contemporaries to sit beside Nadia at the students' table. At first he feels a little out of place; he knows how patronizing it is to act youthful — and dorky to act old — but the high-spirited wine-guzzling young musicians don't seem to mind his presence. Nadia joins in the mirth, but she also sets herself apart. Clearly, she is curious about him and not the least bit shy with her own questions.

I tell her I'm an author, and that I used to play piano for relaxation, but I wasn't very good. I also tell her where I stand, so to speak, in the aftermath of a failed marriage, but I realize right away that she can't relate to a word of it. My predicament is beyond her experience — divorce is not a word in her vocabulary. To her, marriage means her parents' marriage, a taken-for-granted rock on which her career is being built.
Nevertheless, she manifests a real empathy for my creativity. For her tender years — she's nineteen! — she understands self-discipline. In Toshkent, she was educated at a conservatory for gifted children, where she practiced

six hours every day, a regimen she still adheres to (tonight's accompaniment was a favor for a friend, not part of her regular concert preparation). Here in the United States, she has had the good fortune to be chosen as a Steinway Artist, which means that she'll appear in endorsements for the renowned piano maker in exchange for having a factory technician on hand at her performances. Six months ago, she signed with a topnotch management agency. They've already given her a stage name: Nadi Valar.

Nadia (she prefers her original name) tells Budge that her first CD is out, a recording of J.S. Bach's "Goldberg Variations." Actually, she recorded it five years earlier when she first came to the United States. It is the signature piece of her repertoire — the piece she performed in Carnegie Hall — and her critical acclaim rests on it, which greatly impresses Budge, for he has heard of its reputation as one of Bach's most technically challenging compositions.

An idea strikes him: would she consider an exchange? He'll send her his most recent book if she'll send him the CD. She responds enthusiastically.

"That would be splendid, Mr. Moss!"

Momentarily, his troubles seem far away. The pain in his broken heart recedes like the din in the restaurant. Basking in wine-hued warmth, he is captivated by this petite dark-haired, dark-eyed prodigy who hardly touches a thing on her plate but manages to down several glassfuls of chardonnay. Despite their age difference, they're on the same wavelength. Budge feels both protective and romantic. He could sit by her side for hours, years if necessary.

It occurs to me that we may hold the key to each

other's future. She'll eventually have to break away from her parents, and at that point I could step in as husband-manager. Surely, gentlemen of a certain age are preferred bridegrooms in the old country. I'll abide by whatever custom is necessary to ask for her hand in marriage. As a sophisticated and still vigorous — not to mention native born — American male, I'd be invaluable to her from both a personal and business standpoint. I could attend to her every need (see that she gets a restful night's sleep, is sexually satisfied, eats properly, is gowned to her best advantage, gets plenty of practice time, has intellectual companionship, etc.) and also ensure that her tours go smoothly. I'd clinch performance deals on her behalf, pave the way for her fame, wait in the stage wings while she plays, vend her CDs afterwards.

The more I think about it, I'm convinced that I'm exactly right for her. As for my own career — well, I've had my time in the limelight. She's a rising star; she'll benefit from my experience. As lover-mentor, I'll defer to her superior talent, while recasting myself as her help-mate in every sense of the word.

The question is — as the hour grows late and the restaurant empties — should I tell her all this now, or wait?

Wisely, Budge decides not to overwhelm her with so huge a plan. He'll need to put the wheels in motion gradually. As they're getting up to leave, he makes the first declaration of what he hopes will be many.

"I'd love to attend one of your concerts," he says unctuously.

"It would be an honor for me to have you attend," she replies in that stiff foreign way of putting words together. "And then there's the matter of our artistic exchange, too."

81

He is thrilled that she hasn't forgotten. She asks for his e-mail and mailing addresses, jots them on a paper napkin, jots her own and tears them off. He finds the very act of dividing the napkin symbolic — a private pact implying they are two halves of a whole.

Driving back to Rock Hall that evening, Budge is in exalted spirits. The following morning, he sends an e-mail.

Nadia, I really enjoyed sitting beside you at the restaurant last night. It has been a long time since I've spoken with anyone about music on the level we did. You strike me as an unusually gifted and dedicated person.

Please accept my sincere good wishes. I look forward to seeing you in a solo performance soon.

He keeps it short and sweet — no point in rushing things, no point in making her nervous. He reminds himself that he is communicating with a person one-third his age. A week later, he gets his reply.

Greetings, Mr. Moss:

I hope you are in good health. Please accept my apologies for not replying to your e-mail letter sooner, for I have been exhaustively busy with exams and auditions all week long.

It was also my pleasure to make your acquaintance in Philadelphia.

With true wishes for your continued good health. Nadia V.

Budge taps the reply button.

Dear Nadia

I was looking up Kyrgyzstan in the local library's world atlas the other day. Like a typical citizen of the United States, I know next to nothing about your country. Perhaps you could teach me more. And Nadia, you don't have to put a V after your name-- you are the only Nadia I know. Also, please call me Budge — "Mr. Moss" sounds too formal. Despite our age difference, I feel we have quite a lot in common. With every best regard,

Budge doesn't specify what he has in common with a 19-year old musical prodigy from Kyrgyzstan. He feels he can't mention their intertwined destiny yet — a rara avis of her ilk is bound to be skittish and elusive. A careful communicator, he will drop hints without dropping bombshells. Obviously, she is not quite up to speed with respect to their joint future. Nor is she a quick replier; in this second instance, she doesn't get back to him for nine days.

Greetings Budge,

I wish you good health and apology. The Curtis office of financial assistance now occupies all of my time. It is annoying to spend so many hours in this line of pursuit, which leaves me bereft of practice and rest. By my reckoning, artistic development should trump any application for financial assistance. In short spare time, then, I am working on the selection and refreshment of several pieces for fall performances (Budapest and Prague in October). For now, I leave you in good health.

So she needs money! All young artists starve, and some older ones too. Emboldened by this kinship, Budge feels compelled to mention his own straightened circumstances. He wants to make sure that she doesn't mistake him for a sugar daddy — not now at least. Later on, of course, after they're united, what is his will be hers — and vice versa.

Hi Nadia,

I know all about the hassles of applying for financial aid, scholarships, grants, etc. The process is extremely time-consuming and frustrating, so I am in full sympathy with you. I trust you'll soon be back on your more direct-ed path.

That's great news about concerts in Budapest and Prague this fall. I wish I could travel to them, but I, too, have limited resources at the moment. To say I'm broke would be an overstatement, but I do have to watch every dollar I spend.

Here's hoping we both have financial success in the future!

Days pass with no reply, then her CD of the Goldberg Variations arrives. Budge devotes several minutes to marveling at her strong slanted handwriting before ripping open the mailer. On the CD box, Nadia's photograph, taken at the time of recording (when she was fourteen) smiles at him beguilingly, her apple-cheeked youthfulness accentuated by glistening black hair and eyebrows. "To Budge Moss, Let there always be Bach," she scrawled along the margin, and below it, her seven syllable name in full.

Acknowledging the arrival and his first listening, Budge can barely contain his newfound infatuation.

Dear Nadia,

I just wanted to thank you for the CD which arrived

this morning. I played it immediately, of course, and was just "bowled over" by your talent! Your interpretation is marvelous — and what a marvelous piece of music it is!

Thanks so much for sending it. I trust the book will arrive at your home soon.

Penny-pincher that he is, he sent the book by media mail — it may not arrive for another ten days. He writes her again, effusing over her artistry and apologizing for not sending the book more expediently. He writes two more missives of praise and appreciation – he is playing her CD on a more or less constant basis now — and only hopes she doesn't think he stiffed her in the exchange.

At long length, she acknowledges receiving his book, for which she duly thanks him, although she tells him that she cannot possibly begin to read it. Right now she is just too busy; it might be a year or more before she can get to it.

A year or more? Budge's authorial pride is deeply wounded. The paperback happened to be his last free copy from the publisher. He had been saving it as a special gift for someone who would really get a kick out of reading it and knowing him. In Nadia, he thought he'd found the perfect recipient.

I realize her time is severely proscribed by practicing and everything else, but when people tell me they're too busy to read, it annoys the dickens out of me, and I make no exceptions. Anybody who's met me knows I write. Wouldn't Nadia want to know firsthand what kind of stuff I write? Even if she only read the first chapter — and reported back to me that she did — I'd be mollified. Here I sit playing her Goldberg Variations over and over, attuned to her every nuance of interpretive artistry, and

what do I get in return? A raincheck on mutual admira-
tion, wasted postage.

September bustles along with incrementally cooler days and plenty of rain. The e-mail correspondence continues sporadically — on Nadia's side, that is, for Budge's replies are dependably prompt. She tells him a bit about her course work at Curtis, yet manages to reveal almost nothing about her personal life. Budge, on the other hand, is quite specific with his observations and impressions. He has gotten on the Library of Congress website to learn more about Kyrgyzstanian culture and history. He has tracked down well-known recordings of the Goldberg Variations — in particular, Glenn Gould's idiosyncratic renditions from the 1950s — so he can compare them with hers (he never fails to tell Nadia he likes hers better). He reads what the music critics have to say. He studies CD liner notes and listeners' reports on Amazon.com. He visits the Curtis Institute website. And he recounts everything he learns in his e-mail's.

What I'm trying to show is that I'm interested in her. I'm flat-out interested in her life and career and perspective. Okay, so she's still a teenager and I'm at retirement age — it doesn't alter the fact that we could be perfect for each other. A contemporary Heloise and Abelard, joined for business purposes as well as pleasure.

Concerned over her lack of response, Budge develops a plan. He will travel to Philadelphia and offer to take her to lunch and the Art Museum afterward. College students, as a rule, won't turn down a free meal — and surely, she can appreciate great art. He'll let her pick the date and time. He'll downplay the whole scenario, present the idea to her casually, as if it doesn't matter whether or not he ever sees her again.

Hi N,

Hey, I'll be passing through Philly one of these days soon, and I thought it would be neat for us to get together — lunch at that same restaurant and later the Art Museum. Care to join me? No problem if you can't.

He's eager to see how the pianistic prodigy will react. Lunch should remind her what an interesting guy he is, and the hallowed ambiance of the museum should make her realize that age is no barrier. If need be, he can tutor her on the spot; he knows some art history. Then, at a judicious moment — perhaps as they stand before the emotionally charged Eakinses – he will ask her outright what she thinks of the husband-manager plan. If he can work up the nerve, that is.

Greetings, Budge:

I would welcome your visit to Philadelphia in the near future, but the only time I am available would be next Tuesday.

Lunch sounds agreeable — my morning practice ends at noon — but I will not be able to go to the museum with you, as I have additional tutelage (in music theory) starting at 2 o'clock.

If this accords with your plans, I will see you, then, a few minutes after twelve at the restaurant.

It has been six weeks. Will they recognize each other? He wishes his memory of her was more precise (her jejune photograph on the CD isn't much help). Recollection of her comes in fragments. Her voice had a slightly nasal quality to it, as if her best sounds were meant to emanate from her fingertips. She had small hands and small feet. And her hair — how could he forget its moussed cascade?

As for the museum, well, maybe another time. Her schedule is full, which is perfectly understandable. She may be intimidated by the thought of viewing art with so worldly a person as himself. He could always tour the collection alone after lunch.

On the designated Tuesday morning, Budge leaves the cottage at nine o'clock in case he is stuck in traffic, which he isn't. He cruises right up through Wilmington and Chester, doesn't take a single wrong turn, and arrives in the vicinity of the restaurant by eleven. It's not a bad commute, he thinks, for lovers living at either extremity.

I could do this once or twice a week, if necessary. We could meet at the restaurant and then go to her dormitory room. I could find inexpensive overnight parking, or perhaps I could just park at her parents' house in the suburbs and take the bus in.

Budge has time to kill, so he maxes the parking meter before strolling six blocks twice on both sides. At length — and with a full bladder — he walks inside the mostly empty restaurant. It's about ten minutes to noon. He is early but he can't help it.

"Table for two by the window, please," he requests of the maitre d'.

"Is the other party with you?"

"No, she's coming later."

"I'm sorry, sir, but I cannot seat you unless the two of you are here together."

Budge reacts haughtily. "And why can't I just sit there and have a drink while I wait for her?"

"I'm sorry, sir, but these are the management's rules."

"Let me speak to the manager!"

"He's not here today, sir."

"I never heard of such a rule."

"I'm sorry, sir. You're welcome to sit at the bar and have a drink while you wait."

If it were any other situation, I'd walk out after telling the guy to stick his stupid rules up his you-know-what, but the restroom visit is pressing. Also, Nadia wouldn't know where I've gone. No, I have to wait for her. I'm stuck.

Emerging from the men's room, Budge selects a barstool with an unobstructed view of the restaurant entrance. He is in no mood to order anything but a glass of water. Noon passes, ten minutes after, twenty minutes after. He is beginning to think he has been stood up. Twelve-thirty, still no sign of Nadia. The choice tables are long occupied. What's the point of waiting around?

On the verge of bolting, he sees her walking through the door. Yes, it's unmistakably her — he's sure even without his glasses. She is wearing a light sleeveless blouse with dark culottes, and her hair is pinned back by a barrette. She looks tiny and thin, with great pools of fire and genius in her eyes. She spots him right away, too.

"My apologies for being late," she offers breathlessly. "I have only just now come from the practice studio."

Clutched in her arms is sheet music entitled, DEBUSSY. She holds out her free hand. It feels small and cool and valuable. He would lean over to kiss her, but the handshake extension keeps him where he is. The wistfulness of her Kyrgyzstanian smile quite melts him.

"It is so very kind of you to wait for me," she says.

His reply is something to the effect that he hasn't

minded waiting at all.

We're led to the last available table — an ill-lit cubby-hole beside a swinging kitchen door. Nadia takes the wall bench; I sit with my back to the waiter traffic. For a few moments, we're both at a loss for what to say. It's as if we're sizing up our age difference and unrelatedness, and wondering how to proceed. I mention how much I've been enjoying her CD — I tell her that I've listened to it at least 25 times. My confession seems to break the ice; within the space of a minute, we both manage to unleash the torrent of words that characterized our previous encounter.

After they order their food — a glass of pineapple juice and a bowl of gaspacho for Nadia, draft beer and chicken salad for Budge — she volunteers some background information on the CD. She hadn't been long in the United States when the contract offer came through. Her family was friendless, near-penniless, and their English wasn't very good. To keep studio costs to a minimum, she recorded all thirty-two Variations in two days. It was the most difficult musical project she had ever undertaken, and she was a nervous wreck.

"But there's no hint of nervousness on the CD," Budge asserts.

"Naturally not! I knew the whole composition by heart. In my profession, one has to do it right or not at all."

Her indignant vehemence startles him. She is a perfectionist, that's for sure. She goes on to explain that practicing six hours a day obliterates the possibility of error. How unlike his own experience, he thinks. Despite the years of devotion to *his* craft, he still delivers to the tune of rejection slips.

It must be nice to be so sure of yourself. Having the

*future mapped out so succinctly, one professional triumph
after another, as if you're building a crowning edifice of
your interpretive achievement. She's got the clout of prodi-
gious talent propelling her. Her youth and innocence
notwithstanding, she's already sage beyond her years.
She focuses on Art, not Life. She can afford to; the map
presents no obstacles.*

*By way of contrast, I daub at Art and wallow in Life,
all the while worrying about next month's rent. For me,
creativity is always a gamble: I feed the quarters but the
row of cherries rarely lines up. No wonder it's hard for me
to discipline myself these days. Six hours, ha! I'm lucky if
I put in two, with frequent self-imposed interruptions such
as checking for e-mail.*

Sitting in the restaurant with tray-toting waiters
whooshing past his back, Budge tries not to feel sorry for
himself. His youth is gone, he might as well get used to it.
His luck may be gone, too. Across the table from him sits
a brilliant nineteen-year-old from Kyrgyzstan. Though she
is approachable and not the least bit shy, her foreign manners regulate the give and take. The formality of their conversation, plus the contrast in age and experience, quite
deflates him; he just can't work up the nerve to ask dis-
arming questions — like will she marry him and let him
be her manager. He sees his unspoken plan for what it is:
a lonely man grasping at a straw. He wishes he were rich,
so he could whip out his checkbook and write her a nice
fat one.

*Here's five thousand dollars for you to apply to this
semester's tuition. No, no, don't thank me! Please accept
it as a token from one music lover to another. As a long-
standing patron of the arts, I understand the necessity of*

*nourishing the body as well as the soul. The only favor I
ask in return is that you drop the "Nadi Valar" moniker
and use your full name, which I find syllabically beautiful.*

Between sips of soup and juice, she continues to talk
about herself. It's as if she's giving an interview now,
playing *wunderkind* to the hilt. The scene strikes him as
generic Morisot or Degas: a gentleman leaning across a
table toward a damsel. A portrait of a timeless transaction:
he's buying lunch and she's prattling prettily. She is telling
him about one of the more difficult Variations, #23, glis-
sandi of chromatic scales flying upwards and downwards
but resolving in the end. It's a short roller coaster of a
piece — only two minutes and six seconds — and as she
describes its intricacies, her fingers unselfconsciously
flutter as her bare arms swing the breadth of an imaginary
keyboard. Budge is utterly charmed, so much so that her
verbal descriptiveness goes wasted. His mind whirls in
febrile reaction.

*She lives and breathes music, it's becoming clearer to
me. Her devotion to craft is absolute. My own devotion is
wavering; I see that I might lack the wherewithal to
intrude in her world. How could I possibly keep abreast of
such an intelligent creature? A patron, yes — if it were
possible — but a day-by-day facilitator, no. Decades my
junior, she's already light-years beyond me. I'd never be
her equal. I'd be huffing and puffing and always trailing
behind. She'd eventually run circles around me, and then
I'd be shanghaied once again.*

But Budge's private doubts don't mean he is not
enjoying himself. Nadia has been well worth the drive to
Philadelphia. No such prodigy blooms in the culturally

arid soil of Rock Hall. Looking around the restaurant, he also takes satisfaction in seeing that there is no other older man at a table with a young woman who isn't too obviously his own daughter. Besides, the chicken salad wasn't bad, although he could have polished off two servings.

At this point, Nadia is wrapping up the interview. She has finished three-quarters of her soup and put her spoon down. Likewise, the glass of pineapple juice is drained to a level where she no longer sips it. She is making broad observations about the dedication necessary to achieve the highest level of musicianship. Describing the rigorous demands of the classical oeuvre, she mentions how difficult it is to avoid the distracting tendrils of American popular culture. In her estimation, the Internet is a primary culprit, along with cable and satellite television. She gives her younger sister as an example: though she is a first-rate clarinetist, she has grown more and more interested in living the life of a normal teenager. If this trend continues, she will give up her music entirely to devote herself to — Nadia wrinkles her nose contemptuously — a boyfriend.

"Are you saying that you don't have one?"

Budge can't help asking the question; he feels he has a right to know.

"A boyfriend? But of course I don't!" Nadia gives an abrupt little laugh. "I haven't the time."

As if on cue, she glances at her watch. "Well, I really must be going. Thank you for lunch and be sure to enjoy your visit to the museum."

He rises with her. Again, she extends her talented — possibly heavily insured — hand. Realizing that a kiss, even a tiny one on the cheek, may be possible, Budge spontaneously grasps her elbow. Nadia recoils visibly.

She doesn't want to be touched. I'm as shocked as she

is. I wasn't really thinking about what I did. I just reached for her in an entirely nonsexual way, but her reaction makes it seem otherwise. Indecent fondling! Call the vice squad!

Could she have a phobia? Does she prefer contact with ivory and ebony exclusively? My husband-manager plan may not work out after all.

It is just a blip, though, in their cordial, if brisk parting. Their final moments together mimic their greeting, much as Bach's Goldberg Variations begin and end with the same aria (the difference being in the artistic interpretation of first and last). Then Nadia turns her shining headful of barretted black curls and walks away, clutching Debussy.

Watching her disappear, Budge tries to remain optimistic. He tells himself that his plan will take more time — maybe years instead of months. He decides to skip the art museum and drive straight back to Rock Hall.

That night he dashes off an e-mail.

Nadia,

Thanks for taking the trouble to meet me for lunch. I felt that we could have talked for hours, and hope we will have occasion to do so before too long.

I admire you for being so committed to your artistry. You are right to resist influences that might distract you. Please remember that you always have a friend and supporter in me. Meanwhile, from the depths of my heart, I wish you all the best.

Two weeks later, her reply arrives, impersonal in its salutation.

Greetings:

I have become extremely busy, and thus will no longer be able to communicate with you via e-mail letter. Please accept this not as a rejection of your friendship, but as an honest appeal to one who understands the demands upon a person in a laborious artistic career.

She must have gotten a boyfriend, Budge thinks. Oh well, he tried.

Chapter 9

On a breezy afternoon toward the end of September, Budge is seated on a lawn chair and pondering the lonely direction his life is taking. Ragu, who seems more spirited now that the hot weather is gone, rubs against his legs affectionately, as if to console him for his latest romantic failure.

"Times are tough," he tells her. "You're the only friend I've got right now."

Recently, he has been confining his one-way conversations to his pet, reasoning that it is more stimulating than talking to himself.

This is the ultimate disgrace for the heartsick, I think — to grow tired of hearing one's own voice. How often I've railed against fate for making the love in my heart so hard to dislodge! I loved without reservation, I loved implacably — and now I can't get rid of it. All those years I took my fill at the trough of love, and now it's a surplus commodity clinging to my body like avoirdupois. It permeates mind and sinew, this pathetic bloatedness that no pill or diet can reduce. I see my non-future with wretched clarity — my heart growing heavier and heavier with this useless love. Elephantiasis of the critical organ — soon I'll be wheeling my heart around in a wheelbarrow.

Obviously, Budge's prose exaggerates the situation. In truth, he's sitting quite contentedly in the back yard, jotting thoughts in his hardbound notebook, enjoying the afternoon and Ragu's repetitive rubbing. He is writing for an audience, he imagines, that will want to hear some original metaphors on the subject of loneliness, and so he crafts them.

In reality, then, life isn't so bad. He's staying fit and healthy, he's well settled-in, and he's easily fulfilling his daily writing quota. Most importantly, he's continuing to reach out to other people. The Friday night potlucks at the Mainstay have been a blessing in this respect. By now, several of his unattached female acquaintances have actually gone to the trouble to read his books. Budge laps up their praise like Ragu laps up milk on a plate. The only problem is that none of these women ring his bell, so to speak. He's not ruling out the possibility, however, that he may have to choose one at some point in the future.

Is Budge being too picky? Given his state of sexual deprivation, it doesn't make sense, but it happens to be true.

Look at it this way (I tell my cat), the woman has got to appeal to me. I'm one day closer to a full, consensual, hands-on relationship — a crazy, happy, gasping, gripping connectedness on a bed that hasn't seen action since I bought it — but I'm biding my time. One of those Mainstay regulars might do in a pinch — but which one? Asking this very question implies a harsh truth: I find none of 'em terribly appetizing.

As Budge writes these lines in his notebook, he is aware of a pretty blonde in a blue swimsuit looking at him. Standing beside the nearest kiosk, she is dandling a naked baby and keeping track of a toddler. Budge smiles and waves. *Nice people live here*, he reminds himself. The woman — mid-30s, he'd guess — waves back in a friendly way.

Well now! This calls for further investigation! Cute and compact, disheveled pixie hairdo, evenly tanned, excellent posture — the total package is instantly pleasing. Like so many young mothers on the beach, she's got her hands full. The toddler comes running up from the water's edge. "Mommy, Mommy, look what I found!" The platinum-ringleted explorette holds out an oyster shell. Patting the child's head, the woman coos wonderment and approval, all the while bouncing the baby.

This fetching maternal tableau causes me to rise involuntarily from my chair. I cross the drainage ditch and amble over. She probably just wants to say hello, maybe ask me a question.

In his past life, Budge wouldn't have gotten up from the chair. It wouldn't have occurred to him to walk over and strike up a conversation with a strange woman just because she looked at him. Most likely, his wife wouldn't have minded, but his sense of propriety would have held him back. Now, none of that matters anymore.

I believe I'm becoming a better human being. Having crossed the ditch, I walk right up to her. Without flinching or feinting, we greet each other.

"Hi," she says. Or maybe I say it first. Either way, one echoes the other.

"I was just looking at your house."

"Yeah, great location, isn't it?" I reply. "I'm renting by the month."

Up close, Budge is affected by her loveliness. Her fulsome bosom, pressed tight by the swimsuit fabric, creates a dewlap at the corner of each armpit, and her bare feet, turned outward, are planted fore and aft in the beach grass so that she is able to balance the heavy baby.

Her friendliness appears genuine. She doesn't know me from Adam, yet she's singling me out for special attention. I'd go a step further: she's regarding me with admiration just for living where I do and being who I am — a beach-dwelling not-bad-looking middle-aged guy. Is this real, or am I imagining it?

Intimidated by Budge's proximity, the baby becomes temperamental, so the woman holds it at arm's length, raising and lowering its chubby torso. She's got excellent upper body strength, he notes. On her finger is an engagement ring and wedding band — how could he miss them? — but they're extraneous to this moment of instant mutual appreciation.

"I was just thinking," the young mother is saying as she resettles the baby on her hip, "what a perfect place your house would be for somebody writing a book."

Budge is stunned. Is she clairvoyant?

"The water, the setting, the sunsets — a writer could be inspired here, don't you think?"

He looks intently into her blue-gray eyes. "Well, as a matter of fact, I *am* a writer."

"No kidding, really?" Her eyes search his. "You're a writer?"

"Yes, I write books."

"Wow! This is amazing! You're a real writer!"

Budge nods affirmatively.

"Before you came over," she says, "I was looking at your house and thinking, 'I'll bet a writer lives there.' Then I saw you sitting out back with that kittycat, jotting in your notebook. I didn't mean to be nosy, but I almost walked over."

"Are you a writer, too?" Budge inquires.

"I wish! I've taken some creative writing classes and sometimes I keep a journal."

"That's a start," Budge interjects helpfully.

"But I just don't have the time, not with these two!"

She laughs, indicating her offspring. "By the way, that's Naomi — she's almost three — and this is Baby Anna, short for Marianna. She's nine months."

"They're both very pretty. I can see they take after their mother."

"And I'm Julie Kleczynski. Spelled just the way it sounds"

"I'm Budge Moss. Budge as in 'We Won't Budge.' Pleased to meet you."

Simultaneously extending his hand, he clasps hers warmly.

"I can't get over it!" she exclaims. "You're just what I imagined you'd be."

"I sit at my desk and type away. Right over there," he says, indicating the window facing the beach. "On my computer. Every day."

For her I'll make my vocational life as graphic as possible. If she's so enamored of writers, she'll appreciate details. Can the woman drought be ending?

"If I lived here," she's saying, "I'd have my desk right beside the window, too, and I'd write about Rock Hall."

"Well, that's exactly what I'm doing."

"This is totally uncanny! You're writing about Rock Hall? What about? The watermen and local characters and such?"

"No, actually I'm writing about a guy who is getting divorced and winds up in Rock Hall."

He wants to add, *a sort of fictionalized account of my life,* but before he can say it, his interlocutor quickly figures this out on her own.

"So you're divorced?" she inquires. "I hope you don't mind my asking."

"Yeah, getting there."

"I'm sorry," she says.

This seems to be the universal response from women whenever I mention my separation. But what are they sorry for? For another woman's actions? For the pain only they can read in a man's eyes? It's as though they're somehow apologizing for their half of the human race — a blanket admission of guilt, implying that they themselves may choose to inflict similar havoc upon an unsuspecting man at some as yet undetermined point. "I'm sorry," they say, as if to commiserate but also to remind me that women can be fickle entities, who'll drop the bottom out of a man's life when he least expects it.

"It's weird," she's repeating. "You're everything I thought you'd be."

"I hope I am."

For months now, Budge hasn't been so encouraged. Instantly, he projects to the future, picturing himself hooked up with her, raising her two lovable little ones as stepdaughters. He is not too old to play daddy — he adores kids. He and Julie could make one together if they choose to. A blue-eyed baby with the writing gene.

"I know it sounds rude and stupid, but I haven't heard of you," she's saying. "What have you written?"

Casually, he mentions the several titles, adding that at least one of them is still in print and may be available at the local bookseller in Chestertown.

"Tomorrow I'll go right over and buy it. I'd love to read what you've written."

"I'd love to have you read it," Budge says.

The word *love*, bantered so disarmingly, already binds them in unspoken ways, he thinks. Physically, they're obviously attracted to each other. Aesthetically, they're on the same page, too. She is married, but what difference does that make? Divorce, the great liberator, can quickly bulldoze such a minor impediment.

"We're staying for the week at a rental condo down by Waterman's Crabhouse," she is saying. "Me, the girls, and Tidbit, our cocker spaniel."

"Well, it sure is a beautiful time of year," Budge says lamely, thinking to himself, *no problem with the dog. I love dogs, too. Ragu doesn't, but we can work things out. That's the modus operandi for any extended family — working things out.*

"My husband is joining us midweek when he gets off work. He's a firefighter."

"Oh, that's good."

Not good at all. All at once, the stream from an imagined fire hose douses me with such force that I'm knocked backward. Figuratively drenched is how I react to this first mention of a husband. Why couldn't she have kept it to herself? Why do all the really attractive women have one?

Outwardly, I do my best to show no reaction. Husband? Okay, I figured as much. It's odd how the mind has a tendency to fast-forward beyond bad news. The main thing is, I'm in the Don Juan mode — any reality check will just have to wait. I'm in the middle of an enchanting encounter on Rock Hall's public beach. No let-downs allowed. Bummer restricted area. She's interested in me and I'm interested in her. To hell with this mid-week-

arriving interloper!

Little Naomi has come back dragging a sand-encrusted towel, which she drops at Budge's feet before wandering off to the water again. Budge picks up the towel and shakes it vigorously.

"Would it help if I spread this like so?" he asks. "That baby must be getting heavy."

Julie bends over, setting Baby Anna on the towel and giving Budge a clear quick glimpse of cleavage.

"That's perfect, thanks! Mommy needs a break."

She's a nursing mother — her breasts are pillow plump, inviting more than eye alone. Milky thoughts cloud my reason. I surmise that it's near feeding time — the baby's getting cranky. I imagine myself in that lucky kiddo's place. Mommy won't make me wait long. She'll take me in her arms and slip the bathing suit strap down, presenting a nipple to my straining mouth. Grunting peacefully, I'll suckle one breast and then the other.

Looking down at the baby squirming on the towel, Budge can't help but marvel at her pudgy beauty as he shifts to a more ironic viewpoint.

Babies! It's been so long since I've studied one. They get such bad press, you'd think they'd be outlawed. Babies are almost always depicted as negative entities and nuisances. They're aborted in restroom toilets. They're kidnapped. They fall out windows. They die sudden deaths in their cribs. They're the foci of custody lawsuits, legislation, religious fanaticism. They contribute to the cruel statistics of disease and drug dependency, inner city crowdedness, shotgun weddings, overpopulation in general.

They're left accidentally in cars with windows rolled up. They're shaken till they're brain-damaged. They arrive in absurd multiples, thanks to fertility treatments. They're bought and sold on thriving black markets. What social ill isn't traceable to babyhood and its appalling ramifications?

While Budge and Julie make a stab at conversation, Baby Anna manages to work her way to towel's edge, where she somehow transfers grass to her mouth and is now choking. With quick athletic grace, Julie scoops up her daughter and inserts a finger in her mouth to clear away what foreign matter she can find. Several blades of grass are thus extracted while the baby howls lustily. Because Baby Anna is squirming so, Budge reaches over to help hold her still.

"I think I see one more to the side of her tongue," he says. "Mind if I try?"

Julie proffers the discomfited but no longer choking baby, and Budge inserts his own finger between her gums.

The silky saliva, the impuissant protesting jaw, the two tender semicircular ridges from which teeth will emerge. The tongue like a little mauve fish, already fugitive and darting with its distressed vocabulary of vowels. My finger probes for the last of the grass and locates it, whereupon I tease it along the liquid lining of the inner cheek and out the now-bellowing orifice.

"Thanks so much."

"No problem. Glad to be of help."

By motherly miracle, Julie placates the baby, and as she rocks and sways and cuddles, she begins telling Budge a little about herself. She lives in a suburb of Baltimore.

104

She is divorced and remarried (this gives Budge an opportunity to briefly expand upon his own marital status). She has a stepson at camp right now — his father will pick him up en route to Rock Hall later in the week. This boy, thirteen years old, is a major problem in her life — not only is he out of control, but also he's extremely jealous of his half-sisters. The stepson's mother, who happened to be Julie's best friend, died of colon cancer at age 35.

Budge listens attentively; he is always on the lookout for plot material. If the people he talked to only knew how he tends to file away the pertinent facts of their lives, they might all clam up. For Budge, true life stories have always been the matrix of his fiction. He will create characters and situations of his own invention, no doubt, but the catalysts of his imagination are real people explaining themselves, sharing their unique slant and unwittingly donating their personalities to the cause of literature.

As he listens, he drinks her in from head to toe, noting with pleasure every facet of her appearance. She could pass for a gymnast, she is so exquisitely proportioned. High on one thigh is a pale birthmark, half-concealed by swimsuit elastic. A fresh mosquito bite reddens the flesh above one knee — she scratches it unselfconsciously. She has put the baby back on the towel — with better results — and all the while she imparts such a bonanza of personal history that Budge wishes he could be taking notes.

She *was* a gymnast, as it turns out — in fact, a Maryland state champion — and when her competition days were over, she continued in the sport by giving private lessons. In college, she took a number of creative writing courses and thought seriously about becoming a novelist, but this guy came along who insisted that she marry him. Which was a huge mistake, for he turned out to be a good-for-nothing layabout who abused her physically. He was a "controlling asshole" — to use her term — and she couldn't get out from under his sway. She started doing drugs, wound up alienating her family and most of her friends, and nearly overdosed right around the time her best friend died. Fortunately, she had the good sense to seek admittance to a rehab program. It wasn't easy, but she stuck with it. She has been clean now for five years.

"For the rest of my life, I'll always refer to myself as a recovering addict," she says.

She looks up at him with riveting earnestness before her mouth breaks into an impish grin that he interprets — or misinterprets — as 90% friendliness and 10% come-on.

"I don't know why I'm telling you all this crap," she adds. "Do you mind hearing it?"

Budge's mind is in overdrive. Outwardly, he is the picture-image of decorum, but inwardly, he is assailed by lustful thoughts.

Imagine her in bed! She'll straddle me like the "horse" or the parallel bars and bounce away on my cock until I beg for mercy. She must know positions I can only guess at. But maybe I can teach her a trick or two myself, since I've got an advantage in years. Together, we'll soar to new heights of sensuality. Both performers and audience, we'll award ourselves gold medals...

Budge is falling hard for this pretty stranger with two little daughters. In the space of ten minutes, she has opened the floodgates of his heart — there's no other way to express it. He gives a silent benison of thanks for the circumstances that brought them together — the cottage, the beach, his vocation that just happens to turn her on, and the timing that appears, for once, to be working with fate and not against it. A woman like Julie Kleczynski is one in a million, he tells himself. Her self-revelation can only be a most encouraging sign.

"My own life story is dull by comparison," he remarks.

She reacts with a wry, "Yeah, I'll bet!"

The toddler and the baby are demanding her attention. She hugs the one, picks up the other. "I've never met a real writer before," she adds, "but I can see that writers make good listeners."

"You're worth listening to," he says. "Not everybody is."

"I'm glad you think so."

Both daughters are whining now. Frantically, Budge is trying to figure a way to invite her to come back again. Could he suggest that she hire a baby-sitter? During nap time, say? What if she came by for just an hour — that is, before her husband arrives?

C'mon, brain! Come up with something original, something that'll impress her enough to make her want to see me again.

"You've made my day," he blurts.

"Well, you've made my *week!*" she replies.

She has a way with words, and her subtextual message is easily decipherable — or is it? Does this chance meeting have potential, or is it just another passing-ships-in-the-night thing? And why are my words so hackneyed all of a sudden?

She's exactly what I need: a younger woman, but not too young.

"I've got a request to make," she is saying. "If I can

107

find a copy of one of your books, would you mind if I dropped by and had you sign it?"

"Why, I'd be delighted!" he beams. "Come before the middle of the week, if you can."

He wonders if she understands what he is hinting at. It's a delicate matter, this business of the returning husband. For the moment, he dares not press it further, as she is giving absolutely no indication of complicity.

"Well, I better be running along," she says. "It was really fun talking with you."

"I hope we meet again," he says.

"That would be nice."

She offers her free hand and he calculates her handshake's *come hither* pressure. It's difficult to tell, but it could be interpreted as promising.

With baby in arm and toddler in tow, Julie walks toward the parking area. As Budge watches her go, he experiences an irrational feeling of possessiveness combined with a yearning that causes his mind to reach an altogether unwarranted conclusion. *Her next child could be mine*, he thinks. It's more than unwarranted, it's preposterous, nay, ludicrous, but that's how he is reacting.

We'd make a fine family of five — six if the stepson wanted to join us (but he'd have to mend his ways). I'd be one of those mature papas — strict, yet loving to a fault. I'd write a bestseller and provide a comfortable home at the edge of Chesapeake Bay — if not here, then somewhere up the line. I'd teach the kids to swim, birdwatch, groove on sunsets, and respect all living things. Childrearing would become second nature to me; I'd excel in patience and helpfulness. As a husband, there'd be no finer specimen anywhere on the eastern shore. Julie would see that she's got a good man, not an absentee loser who doesn't cherish her the way she deserves.

In the coming days, Budge is hotly inspired to write down everything he can to further this scenario.

One afternoon midweek, there's a knock on the screen door. I'm just finishing up the dishes — I've been keeping the cottage spic-and-span in anticipation of her arrival. I've already emptied the trash, dusted the windowsills, picked up my clothes, changed the sheets. I want to make a good impression.

It's Julie. Alone. She must've read my thoughts, my cornucopia of fantasies.

"I apologize for dropping by so unexpectedly. I hope I'm not interrupting your writing."

With a laugh, I assure her she's not. Should I tell her a writer's best-kept secret? That writers never write full-time. Usually, we write in short bursts — maybe three or four hours total in twenty-four — but we con the world into thinking that we're slaving away at our craft, coaxing the reluctant words onto the page in nonstop fashion, wringing our imaginations dry. Nah, I better keep it to myself. A little fictive mystery adds to the authorial allure.

"I'm so damn glad to see you! I was hoping you'd come back."

"Really?" she asks, looking up at me, squinting.

"Really and truly," I elaborate.

"Then I'm glad, because I needed to get away from the little ones," she says. "They're both napping. I'm free for at least an hour. Playing mommy 24-7 gets to be too much sometimes."

"I can imagine. Is your husband here yet?"

"He's supposed to arrive around suppertime. At which point, I'll have to deal with him, too."

She rolls her eyes to illustrate exactly what she means. Clearly, she is not the least bit excited by his arrival; rather, she's dreading it. Right now she's serious about taking a break from her familial responsibilities.

"Well, come in and sit down," I say, but somehow my words trigger a guilty response.

"I can't stay long. I just wanted to see you again. I want to see where you work, too."

I usher her to the room where my desk is. Dictionary, thesaurus, notebook, scraps of paper all over the place, and at the center, my trusty laptop, currently clammed shut. My little plexiglass-based thermometer reads 74 degrees. Beside the desk is a wastepaper basket (oops, forgot to empty it) and a crate upon which my moody old printer sits. Atop the printer are my binoculars, ready to scrutinize the estuarine birds or babes.

"This is neat! I've never seen a real writer's workspace."

"Yeah, well, it's no big deal. I'd tell you that I get my inspiration from looking out at the water, but I'd be lying. Between me and the water, as you see, is the portajohn."

Julie laughs, but then she turns serious. "I'd give anything to live in a place like this."

"What's it like where you live?"

It's the logical question for me to ask — not that it matters, but perhaps she wants to tell me.

"The very opposite of this. Suburbia at its blandest. No view, no peace and quiet. Obnoxious neighbors. Lots of traffic noise from the beltway."

She exhales audibly, as if ridding herself of thoughts of home. Introspectively, she stares out the window. Then she turns her attention to my assortment of recently accumulated thrift store furnishings. Everything's got a patina of dereliction, everything's got a past longer than a future.

Can she see that I'm poor, that I'm scraping by on the nostalgia of broken dreams?

"I love this place. I love the way you furnished it."

It's my turn to say, "Really?" I'm incredulous that somebody of a generation after mine and several increments beyond my tax bracket can appreciate this stuff.

"You're creative," she says. "That's what I don't have at home — creativity. Everything's cut and dried, everything's as it's supposed to be, nothing's out of place, not even in the girls' bedrooms. You can't imagine how boring it is."

I barely suppress an ironic chortle. "Well, if you knew how hard I've been working to get this dump squared away, you might compliment me for neatness, too."

We both laugh at my joke. The tension — what little there was — disappears entirely. Continuing with the house tour, I motion toward the doorway across the hall. Grandly (and thoroughly facetiously) I announce, "And here's the bedroom!"

"Are you giving me a hint?" she asks with a sly squinting grin.

"Well, not exactly, but if you want..."

"Oh, but I do want. I want what you want. It is what you want, isn't it?"

Great God almighty! Are my ears deceiving me? Is she suggesting what I think she is? Is my sexual quarantine ending at last?

"Are you saying that we..."

"Well, why not? Only we'd have to do it quickly."

Oh, I've waited and waited and waited for this nudge! This green light! It is unmistakably green, isn't it? I haven't gone color blind, have I? The suddenness quite takes my breath away. The initiative having fallen into my lap, I realize that it's up to me to match her boldness with

111

my own. I look her straight in the eye and say, "Julie, I want you and I've wanted you from the very first moment I saw you."

I take both her hands in mine. Little tanned paws with tapering digits, expensive-looking rings, nice nails.

"I've thought about you every day and dreamed of you at night," I add for good measure.

"I haven't stopped thinking about you either," she says. "Now you know what I came for."

Her wantonness is hard to figure out. Is it my gray-beard masculinity — ahem! — or does she have other reasons? Like she's a swinger or a nympho or she's tit-for-tatting her husband's infidelity. Or perhaps it's a spontaneous, sperm-of-the-moment thing. Well, if it's out of the blue, so be it! Stranger things have happened between strangers. What I'm unprepared for, however, is a true-life encounter that so perfectly matches my fantasy. This is new territory for a writer who's had no sex in a very, very long time. I had no idea it would happen this expeditiously.

"But we have to hurry," she reminds me again. "I need to be home in an hour."

She follows me into the bedroom. The stopwatch is ticking.

"May I undress you?" I ask tentatively.

Julie laughs. "Oh, let's not bother with all that. Let's just get down to business."

She's wearing a T-shirt, shorts, and sandals. No bra under the T-shirt, which she quickly pulls off. God, her breasts are beautiful! She unbuttons the waist of her shorts and slips them down, then peels off her pink panties just as quickly. Lastly, she kicks off her sandals. She's a paragon of tan-lines, pale-fleshed where it matters most. Proportionally gifted and completely uninhibited, she stands before me ready for sexual intercourse.

I've been shedding my own clothing as quickly as possible, and now I'm naked as well, with an erection that's achieving full strength by visual stimulation alone. Two people newly bare-assed to each other in full daylight — it's almost shocking! Tentatively, we draw closer. Like automatons, we're programmed to engage each other. We've come this far, we might as well keep going. We bump and then lock. The fact that she is so much shorter than I am gives us an almost awkward imbalance. My arms want to draw her upward, while her arms wrap themselves around my lower back. Her breasts and my penis press into our respective stomachs. I crane my neck way down and she tilts her face way up, and thus we manage our first kisses.

"Mmm, this is nice."

"Sure is."

"You seem good and ready."

"You make me that way."

I'm thinking I was fortunate to have changed the sheets on the bed. Recently, I've become lazy about doing the laundry, despite the washer and dryer being right in the middle of the kitchen. Somehow, they escape my vision and the laundry basket grows mountainous. Today, though, I'm completely caught up — everything's washed, dried, folded, and put away. Aside from our clothes that just now fell to the floor, there's no mess to speak of, not even a stray sock.

Our height difference soon becomes negligible as our mouths turn into rubbery wet canyons to explore. Her lips taste like cinnamon — cinnamon portals to her very soul — and between these explorations occur random anointments, even as our fingers exchange random strokings. I bend down to kiss her frontally, beginning with the soft

113

swelling that rises from her ribcage to the semi-pendant orbs that women always refer to as their "boobs," finally concentrating on the aureole itself with its hard little cork of an epicenter. Mouthing her nipples, I suckle each one just enough to draw a spritz of sweet human milk (Julie's encouraging hands caressing the back of my head tell me this is okay). I don't mean to rob the baby, but I need to taste for myself what this lactating lover is all about. To call it a turn-on falls short of its aphrodisiac description. What sublime nourishment! What grace, what communion!

And she gives as well as she gets. I'd almost forgotten the sharp sensation of a heartfelt penile squeeze (she makes it stick out in front of me like an iron flange). She strokes my buttocks until they're aflame. I haven't felt so engorged in months. Panting with lust, I gather new physical strength. Now all hurdles seem possible to leap over. My brain stops churning; I no longer think, for example, about the laundry. Her touch eases my mind even as it excites my senses. Deliberateness is the key: devouring one another calmly and digesting every tingle.

"Come lie down," I whisper hoarsely.

Flushed and gasping, she lets me topple her. Supine, we're more equally sized because our heads share the pillow. Arms flung across each other, we scrutinize each other's face close-up, smiling tentatively. Her skin and hair are radiating lavender and castille — possibly mingled with another perfume — overlayering a musk of sexual readiness. My hand drifts down across her soft stomach, testing her navel's depression, patting the mat of her pubic hair with my palm as my fingers gently prod the goal between her legs.

"Wait a minute," she gasps. "We ought to ask each other some questions."

114

"You mean about protection and STDs and herpes and all that?"

"You're reading my mind," she laughs.

"For me, no STDs, no herpes, but I haven't got any protection either."

"Same here. I'm not ovulating, that's for sure, so I guess everything's okay."

Mouth to mouth, a new suction emboldens her kisses. She wants me inside her now. She parts her legs incrementally so I can stroke her vulva, my fingers working their way into the hot liquid infinity of her vagina. God, is she ready! No K-Y jelly needed! But I'm not going to consummate the sex act quite yet; I want to taste one more of her flavors. Kissing her along the route my fingers so recently explored, I kneelingly reposition myself at the lower end of the bed so that my face is between her legs. As my tongue lightly flicks her clitoris, the pressure of her thighs on my ears tells me I'm doing the right thing, and if that weren't enough, the way she jerks her head from side to side indicates, I think, that she's almost ready to come. I raise my head from the muffy dankness.

"Do you like that?" I ask.

She answers with her forearms, which, as I have previously noted, are exceptionally strong. She tugs at me now; she's had all she can stand of foreplay. As she draws me upward, my penis slips inside her almost as an afterthought. Thus we begin that one-on-one reckoning that makes the world a livable place.

A hallmark of satisfactory lovemaking is when a man's lips impart to a woman's lips the flavor of her own cunt. Deep and highly seasoned kisses are what she apparently relishes, too. Our fusion is nothing short of a miracle; I probably should be pinching myself — is this really happening? From strangers on the beach to partners in bed

115

seems the stuff of televisionland, yet here we are, fused and fuzed, on the verge of detonation. Much as I'd like to prolong it, this frenzied mouth-to-mouth, groin-to-groin contact can only last so long — one or the other of us will surely burst. Perhaps sensing this, she breaks away for air.

"Wait a minute," she gasps. "Let me get on top. Hurry!"

I withdraw to a kneeling position, while she pulls up her knees and scoots out from under me. Obediently, I roll over on my back. Now superior, she lifts one leg to straddle me, a mattress arabesque that I help to steady by gripping her hips. She rises on her haunches to impale herself on my erection, grunting as I slide within her. I have to will myself not to ejaculate during this procedure; the oblique angle of penetration creates exquisite pressures which, combining with her gyrations, minimize my last vestiges of control.

But control myself I do, because I want to behold her from this position. Her compact foreshortened body is performing again, as of old. Above me, she rises and sits, rises and sits, her breasts lolling fetchingly, her hands gripping my armpits. Like a wild mare, she tosses her head, completely giving herself to the pleasure she both experiences and creates. Her breathing is measured and sharp — I can feel the exhalations lightly buffeting my chest and shoulders. Tenderly, I grab for her breasts, as if to spur her on; then, with more force, I clutch at her bottom, sinking my fingers in its pliant mass. She's doing all the work now. My pelvis is passive for the most part because I don't want to interfere with whatever she's accomplishing for herself clitorally.

She's so wrought up that she comes before I do, which is a first for me. In my experience — which is by no means slight — women either don't come at all, or fake it, or resort to fingering (or battery-operated appliance), or manage to come eventually in a great grinding ballyhoo — a sort of Olympian assertion of sexual equality. Julie does none of these. All along, she's been working linearly toward her goal, eliminating the competition (or inertia) along the way, and now that she's there, she's bawling "oh, oh, OH, OOOHHH!" Her involuntary spasms set off my own payload. Ahhh, I have no choice! Yet our mutual St. Vitus dance, ripping as it is, gives me a distinctly ancillary feeling. My semen fills her cunt not by poking and plundering, but by persuasion. She draws the life-stuff right out of me — more extraction than explosion. And I'm not complaining; I'm sure this is the way consensual sex was meant to be.

Stillness engulfs us now for the better part of five minutes. Her hands leave my armpits as she uprights her torso. I'm the hull and she's the conning tower. She's peering down at me with that sly grin. Wordlessly, I grin — or perhaps grimace — back at her. She doesn't have to ask if it was nice and I don't have to ask either. Still conjoined, we form a tableau of intermingled thoughts and body fluids. The peacefulness is profound. I'm thinking I could really love this woman, were she mine. I could appreciate her, worship the sandals she walks in and the bathtub she bathes in, donate an organ to her if necessary. What we accomplished is the most commonplace of endeavors, yet we've brought something new to bear: a surprise compatibility, awesome in its promise. Ours is an accidental friendship that now means more to me than anything else in life. I want her and her children (and her parents if necessary) to come and live with me. I want to give her another child if she wants one — we'll make it just the way we made this (childless) miracle.

Sending a final shudder through my loins, she rolls

expertly off me, taking care not to put her weight on my legs.

"What time is it?" she asks.

I reach for my watch on the bedside table. "Half-past four."

"Uh oh, Mommy needs to be going."

She strides to the bathroom to wash up, and I sit on the edge of the bed in a daze. How can I tell her that she has to alter her life's course and I have to alter mine? How can I tell her that what matters is us — building a new life together from scratch. Hubby'll just have to bow out as gracefully as he can. Who is he, what's he like? I don't give a hoot. Will he understand that he needs to let her go? He has no choice. Will she understand? I hope so.

"Gotta run!"

She yanks up her panties, puts on her shorts and T-shirt, slips into her sandals, fluffs her hair. I'm still fumbling with my underwear.

"Will you come back?"

That's all I dare to ask at this point.

"Sure," she replies. "I'll bring a book for you to autograph, if I can find one."

She takes three steps in my direction, rising on tiptoes to give me a quick hard kiss that just misses my mouth, and then she's out the door.

Thus Budge taps out his imaginative version on the keyboard, wholly untrue. But he is writing fiction, so it can be expected. Real life, as usual, is sadly lacking in sexual fulfillment.

This is what actually happens: the week goes by and Julie never shows up. Mulling her absence, Budge considers several possible reasons. Maybe she never intended to come back. Or maybe she did, but now it's impossible with her husband on the scene.

Maybe she talked herself out of returning. Maybe her husband talked her out of it.

Budge clings to the hope that she will reappear. She was so sincere, so understanding, so intent on acquiring a book of his and reading it. Only gradually does he realize his folly: his mind is making too many anticipatory leaps, as usual. How can a ten-minute conversation with a stranger on a beach result in relational nirvana? It can't, he knows damn well it can't. So why has he gone to such great lengths to build this love-castle in thin air? This one and all the others?

My situation smacks of desperation. I thought it would be an easier transition from marriage to remarriage — I mean, playing nuptial chairs is no earth-shattering event, is it? Everybody's doing it. You lose one, you find another. But here I am, months later, finding no one, yet more determined than ever, and so my brain kicks into over-drive. I'm connecting the dots where there are no dots to connect. Desperation is the handmaiden of determination (or is it the other way around?).

But exactly a week later, when he is at his desk trying to propel this disjointed first-person account forward — and not having an easy time of it – he is aware of several vehicles idling outside the cottage. Pickup trucks or SUVs, by the sound of them. Perplexed, Budge hits the save ikon. Has there been an accident? He heard no crash. Just as he is getting up to investigate, there comes a rap on the screen door.

"Hi! Remember me?"

It's Julie. She is holding her youngest and a book.

"Of course I do. It's so good to see you. Won't you

come in?"

"Can't stay but a minute," she says, indicating the waiting caravan. "We're on our way home."

In her T-shirt, shorts, and sandals, she is the spitting image of his fantasy. "I managed to locate a copy of one of your books," she's saying. "Would you mind signing it?"

"I'd be happy to."

Budge would detain her, even for a few precious seconds, to get a good look at her again. Gratitude wells up within him — she came back, just as she promised.

"Please, c'mon in. I'll fetch a pen. And while I'm at it, let me give you a quick tour of the cottage. This is the kitchen and living area, over there's the bedroom — where the headlights wake me up at night — and here's where I write."

Jiggling the baby, she nods approvingly at his desk by the window and the view of the bay behind the portajohn. Outside, there is a rude blast of a horn. Budge grabs a desktop pen to inscribe the frontispiece. *To Julie Kleczynski in true friendship, Budge Moss.*

"How nice! Thank you," she says. "Well, I've got to be going."

The horn blasts again.

"Oh, that jerk!"

Budge finds her reference to her husband comforting. He probably *is* a jerk.

"So it was nice meeting you and all that. Maybe we'll run into each other next year."

Julie takes three steps in his direction, rising on tiptoes to give him a quick hard kiss that just misses his mouth, and she is out the door.

Chapter 10

*As cooler weather arrives, I've begun walking more.
Midday and evening as well as morning. In the environs of
Beach Road, I'm probably known as The Stroller — or
perhaps The Prowler — because I'm so often stepping out
for a breath of fresh air. This monastic life combines work
and solitude seamlessly, and I must admit that my writing's coming along well — in this respect, I can pat myself
on the back — but my bachelorhood remains abysmally
bereft of female companionship. I'd give almost anything
to find a lover, one I can positively relate to.*

While the veracity of Budge's ultimate statement is
beyond reproach, his penultimate one isn't exactly true (of
course, it's understood that he is writing fiction, so he's
excused). He has made one good friend, an elderly lady
who lives seven blocks away — also on the water. Her
name is Sue Baskin and she has been in Rock Hall for
longer than anyone can remember.

Sue, age 92, is — to put it bluntly — a wrinkled old
prune, but one with an aura of such kindness and concern
that it's easier to visualize her as a ripe plum. Right from
the start, Budge pegged her as a worthy acquaintance. She
was sitting in her porch rocker one afternoon when he was
walking past, and she called to him in such a friendly manner that he came over and introduced himself. She then
followed up her amiable quizzicality with an invitation to
tea, and poor Budge, flattered by the attention — and fam-
ished as usual — was only too glad to oblige. They sat and
talked for nearly three hours as their friendship took root.

He ate more chocolate chip cookies that afternoon than he had eaten all year.

Having appraised Budge's loneliness over the subsequent weeks, Sue has taken it upon herself to be thoroughly supportive (she herself may be termed lonely, but in an altogether different way, having buried two husbands, the last some fifteen years ago).

She's a heavyset woman with thinning white hair, a mouth that's glibly mobile, and eyes behind granny glasses that belie either amusement or merriment — I'm not sure which. She retains a dependable memory, has excellent hearing, drives a car (an Escort about the vintage of my Corolla), and has no qualms about saying what's on her mind. At present, she is the most unselfish, unstressed-out, at-peace-with-herself person I know.

As it is, Sue is known to nearly everybody in Rock Hall, and those who don't know her on a first-name basis, know her by sight. She is one of the town's enduring institutions; she spearheads fund-raisers, volunteers at fire hall benefits, collects food for the needy, and is an ever-present participant at any gathering of civic boostership. Credentials like these make her eminently suited to tackle the plight of Beach Road's literary arriviste. For all his obtuseness, Budge recognizes her worth.

The friendship also happens to be evolving at a significant moment, because Budge is pretty much burned-out on the Mainstay potlucks.

On Fridays, I've been coming for the food, not necessarily for the company. I know it sounds antisocial, but once a week I'm so glad to go off my budget-conscious diet (beans, greens, turkeyburgers, more beans) that I heap my plate and stuff myself silly. Only as an after-thought do I consent to chitchat (the bores vastly outnum-ber the interesting folk). The women, as a rule, have more to talk about than the men, so I tend to place myself exclu-sively in their midst. But as I said earlier, all the women who really appeal to me are married. I've made some progress with the few — very few — unmarried ones I find both visually and verbally tolerable, but not enough to sat-isfy me or — apparently — them. They're either absurdly reticent or aggressively forward. There seems to be no middle ground. I would hazard a guess that these women have come to Rock Hall for the same reason I have — washed up and broken hearted — and they're probably lonelier than hell. Yet for some reason, they don't react to me the way they react to Dr. So-and-so, the retired dentist with a paunch like a wrecking ball and the conversation of a wet blanket. They worship his fat old ass, whereas I bring out the worst in them. They know me by name, they've read (or are reading) my books, but any attraction between us seems destined to never reach a critical mass.

Budge's newfound friendship with Sue Baskin is the preferred alternative. Far from being put off by her great age, he finds it comforting. He can express himself with-out feeling intimidated by the outcome. He can actually make conversation without struggling to present himself as some kind of ideal man. Formerly dismissive of elder-ly females, he is now changing his tune.

It's not just that I'm not interested in her. I regard her more as a person than a woman. Sue and I don't have to construe that our relationship may lead to "involvement" — one look at her tells me this is impossible. Her face is a corrugated liver-spotted rictus of desuetude. Her general shapelessness, with flesh pendent under her chin and fore-arms, quite repels me. "Spry" is too kindly an adjective, implying the worse (like "articulate" or "veteran"). Slow of step, diminished by osteoporosis, talkative to the point of rambling, Sue remains in this world by dint of survivor-ship. Despite the manifold hardships I surmount, I'm nowhere near the survivor she is.

She's old enough to be my great-grandmother! (No, no, I take it back — not that old, but you know what I mean.) She ran out of sex appeal — or it ran out on her — I would estimate, a good thirty years ago. Not that I'm a connoisseur of aged females, but I do think I can extrapo-late with reasonable accuracy that she was quite good-looking in her youth. The echo faintly reverberates in the way she still assumes that others take notice of her. From what I gather, she's had a long, family-filled life, but everybody is either dead or moved away. For the past fif-teen years, she's been living by herself with four para-keets, with whom she unabashedly communicates.

Because of Sue's many connections, she is also some-thing of a matchmaker. With adroit questioning, she has grasped Budge's situation and sorted through the possibil-ities right in the neighborhood. Through her, he has met Winifred B., whose boyfriend recently passed away from chronic wasting disease. He has met Mildred F., who, though ten years his senior, is actively seeking a replace-ment husband (the old rogue took up with a younger woman). He has met Jocelyn A. and Tillie Z., both school-teachers, friendly enough, but whose sexual preferences are not altogether clear (if he's up for that kind of chal-lenge). Plus, there are any number of more distantly habi-tated single women who've just happened to drop in at tea time.

Sue would be only too happy to make more introductions, but nothing seems to pay off. Like the women who come to the Mainstay with their hopeful casseroles and bottles of cheap Australian wine, Budge finds them lacking in one aspect or another. With what passes for a rakish laugh, he shrugs off Sue's offers of further assistance. He'll get lucky one day, he assures her.

In the meantime, he continues to stop by her house. He knows that she is always there and always glad to see him. He feels he can trust her.

At least twice a week, I knock on her door. She's told me that she prefers I don't phone ahead of time, which is fine with me. My visits break up the monotony of her day sitting in a chair reading the newspaper and listening to NPR. "Come right on in!" she'll call cheerily, and the invitation itself is a reward. In the neighborhood, she's become my lodestar, my guiding spirit. I find myself telling her things that I would never tell anyone else. No, I don't cry on her shoulder, or anything like that, but I do tend to get confessional whenever we talk at length. This past Tuesday, I blurted out how I missed a sex life.

Now why would I confide that to a 92-year-old? What on earth possessed me? In light of my cavalier brush-off of her latest offer of introduction, it must have sounded particularly pathetic. I could just as well have said that I was climbing the walls, that I jerked off twice a week but it didn't do any good.

A sudden ache of celibacy possessed me, and the words just tumbled out. I felt so stupid! But she just looked at me through those granny glasses that magnify her twinkling eyes and said, "It won't be long now."

Whether she was a Delphic oracle or just saying the first thing that came into her mind, her words soothed my poor downtrodden heart. All at once, my courage soared and I was filled with hope. "It won't be long now." How I wanted to believe her! She spoke as if it were a statement of fact, not just a prediction. Soon I would be exiting this tunnel of loneliness and limited resources. Soon I would be accepting and reciprocating another's love. When that glorious moment came, I'd reenter the world a humbler person, so that by my own example I could show others that rock bottom is never the end but always the beginning, a springboard to betterment.

It's no exaggeration to say that with that simple phrase, Sue turned my life around. When it was time to go, I went over and gave her a big hug.

"What's that for?" she asked, flustered but obviously pleased.

"For saying nice things. For being my friend."

"What did I say? Oh, you mean that business about your eventually finding somebody? Well, it's true, Budge. You're a very attractive man!"

I sincerely hoped she wasn't implying that she had designs on me. The idea was worrisome. Had she misread my comradely embrace? Did she think I was into gerontophilia? Fearing the worst, I headed out the door as quickly as possible. Surely, she understood that I didn't want to get physical — God forbid if I gave her that impression! — but I couldn't tell for sure. Back at the cottage, hindsight got the better of me. Why had I hugged the old broad so fiercely? My action was totally uncalled for. She said a few kind words, and I overreacted.

Mr. Impulsive screws up again! Sue Baskin — of all people — thinks I've got the hots for her, and now I've got to deal with that issue as well as everything else.

Filled with at least a paragraph of inspiration, Budge

makes his fingers patter busily upon the keyboard.

Women! Always my weak point! Here I am, a 55-year-old guy who's been around so many times that it's ridiculous. I'm too damn interested in women — that's my problem. Invariably, it leads me to do and say the wrong thing. Why can't I just take an emasculating pill or potion? Lose this perpetual preoccupation once and for all. Other men my age concentrate on luxury cars, boats, stock portfolios, swimming pools. Or drink — lovely edge-dulling alcohol that eases ravelments and encourages karioke. But no, not me — I'm above such pursuits. All I want is female flesh — all flavors and colors and sizes and shapes. I want to gorge myself, I want to devour Women with a capital W. My unrequited nerve-endings cry out for gratification. In my boxer shorts, my penis flops around like a disconsolate eel. I can't take much more of this horniness. I beg the medical profession for help — surgical, pharmaceutical, psychological, whatever. I am your guinea pig, I am your laboratory rat. Get me out of this inane phantasmagorical rutting rut before it's too late!

While Budge's prose liberally flies away with itself, he remains more or less inert at his desk. His financial survival is linked to his word output; he needs to finish this writing project and get started on another. The sailboat money is running out. Nights are turning chilly, although the leaves on the trees are still green. He looks out to the water, ignoring the portajohn (it was tipped over by vandals this past weekend and righted only after he notified the Rock Hall police). fewer sailboats are heading out to the open bay, and of their number, only one or two have raised sails. This is the time of year when weekend sailors take to the water only briefly, more intent on hauling their craft ashore for maintenance followed by long-term storage.

I was told by the rental agent when I moved here that beach activity would lessen after Labor Day. I figured that the quietude would descend all at once — everybody would just pack up and go home. Well, it hasn't happened so abruptly. Sunny weekends continue to draw beachgoers; picnickers occupy the tables and kiosks. Sunset clubbers and stray bicyclists still arrive for the end-of-day spectacle, although it's earlier now and not so conveniently delayed after suppertime. During the week, however, the parking spaces are mostly empty and the sign forbidding beach use between dusk and dawn is inadvertently obeyed.

In the course of one afternoon's visit, Sue Baskin invites him to stay for dinner. A week earlier, she asked if he liked Maryland blue crabs, and when he said he wasn't sure, she took it as a sign that he needed some culinary initiation. Now she has caught several of the crustaceans off her bulkhead and wants to share them with him. He gratefully accepts her invitation, but insists on going to the liquor store to fetch a bottle of wine.

It has been a long time since he was a dinner guest — not since he left the western shore.

I don't care if she's nineteen or ninety. If a woman invites me for a meal, I won't turn her down.

To his credit, Budge has gotten over his apprehensions about Sue. Subsequent visits have shown that his elderly friend has no designs on him other than to help him achieve a level of social comfort so that he no longer has to think of himself as an outsider. That and, of course, the matchmaking. If anything, her string of unsuccessful introductions have bolstered his self-confidence. As a result of them, he is finally allowing himself to imagine that he may be more in demand than he had previously thought possible.

Nevertheless, Sue continues to occupy Budge's writer-ly thoughts.

She offers a no-strings companionship that a single guy can handle — no hidden agenda, no wishful outcome, and, above all, no sexuality waiting in the wings. She's just a friend, one that can be counted on. Moreover, she's not a surrogate mother and I'm not a surrogate son. When we're together, Sue and I treat each other as equals.

How refreshing true friendship is! She and I have a surprising amount in common. We both love Beach Road for what it's not. We'd rather look at the water than sail on it. We chuckle over local inanities, like the post-midnight street sweeping truck that wakes up the neighborhood. We agree about so many things that we occasionally fall silent for minutes on end, lost in tandem contemplation.

As ancient as Sue is, she no longer has to prove or improve herself. She leads a life of blissful indifference, though on another level, she's alert and opinionated. In her company, I find myself taking mental notes; I want to be just like her when I'm an nonagenarian.

Well before dark, Budge returns to her house with the bottle of wine. He has taken his time because he is cognizant of her own slowness – she is never in a rush, not even when the phone is ringing or the kettle is whistling.

He finds her at the edge of the bulkhead, hauling up — with some difficulty — a crab trap tied to a length of rope.

"I just caught three more," she calls to him. "We'll

have a feast tonight!"

The preparation for the feast turns out to be a complicated procedure, beginning with the locating of the steaming pot which, as luck would have it, is buried beneath a pile of rusty tools in an adjacent shed. As far as Budge can tell, the pot hasn't been used in years — nor have the tools. The inside of the pot is barnacled with mud-dauber nests and sticky white cocoons of indeterminate insects in the larvae stage. Utilizing scrub brush and garden hose, he scours it thoroughly before filling it with fresh water.

After carrying the heavy, sloshing pot to the waterside deck, his next task is to change the outdoor cooker's propane tank, which is empty. The spare tank is underneath the back porch — at least Sue thinks it is — and so another search ensues. The spare, it turns out, is hidden beneath an overturned wheelbarrow, where it has lain for a decade or more, judging by its dirtiness, but appears to have some gas left in it. Budge hefts the tank to the cooker and fastens the hose, not omitting to extricate the dry leaves and cobwebs from the grille before he ignites the burner. After putting the water on to boil, his next job is to fetch the crabs.

I can see how grateful she is for my assistance. The crabs don't go gently; I repeatedly bang the trap on the deck to get them out. Only reluctantly do they drop into the waiting pail — have they an inkling of their fate? The other crabs have been in the refrigerator for a day or two, so they aren't nearly as feisty. Still, I take the precaution of using tongs. Then another lengthy search: somewhere on the shelves of her pantry is a can of Old Bay seasoning. Eventually, it turns up, but it's caked so hard that I have to devote a good ten minutes chopping at it with a table knife. Following this, I help her locate the crab-picking tools. These turn out to be irretrievably lost, so we settle for pliers and a hammer from her late husband's tool chest.

She tells me that she hasn't cooked crabs in ages, and I believe her.

Waiting for the water to boil, Budge and his hostess occupy deck chairs and sip the wine he has brought — cheap, but French. It's remarkable how relaxed he can get in Sue's presence; unrestrainedly, he babbles on about anything that comes to mind. There isn't much in life that Sue hasn't experienced, and she listens with a sympathetic ear. As the sun sets, he keeps their glasses full. Finally, at her suggestion, he checks the pot, having risen somewhat unsteadily to his feet. The water is half boiled away. He dumps in the crabs, quickly placing the lid over their demise.

Sorry guys! Can't be much fun for ya. Rest assurred, however, that you're going to a good home — my stomach.

But Budge has scant opportunity to ponder the crustaceans' fate. Once he is back in his chair, his attention is fully absorbed by his elderly friend.

The more we communicate, the more I realize that our age difference is meaningless. Sure, we're almost forty years apart, but somehow it's not relevant to the ebb and flow of our conversation. The rapport between us just glides along. If she occasionally repeats herself, I let it pass, knowing that my own head is spinning and I am probably guilty of the same. I haven't enjoyed such a wine buzz since my wife and I were together, back in the days when we'd sit on the patio with a bottle between us, map-

ping out home improvment projects and holiday plans.

I scrutinize Sue's face as she talks. Her merry magnified eyes peer back at me, and her chin bobs like a puppet's, loosely attached to the rest of her features. Is she watching me watch her? Now she grins, and her cheekbones stand out like apples as her temples crinkle. She makes a droll point — the years haven't dulled her funnybone — showing her uneven yellow row of upper teeth (she grew up before the era of orthodonture).

Her great age gives her a lighthearted authority. I hang upon the import of her every tongue-in-cheek pronouncement. I'm in the presence of someone who can see a lot more humor in life than I can right now.

Having finished his bottle, they opt to open a bottle of hers, a not-bad Argentine shiraz which — at her bidding — he totters to the kitchen for. The fresh glassfuls ensure continuity between deck chair and dining table, between past life and present. Hostess and guest are soon off on another conversational tangent, but suddenly he remembers that he better check the crabs.

They're done — well done — red and redolent and ready to crack open. One by one, he transfers them to a serving platter and brings them to the newspaper-covered table. Sue has prepared pickled beets and cole slaw in advance — these he sets upon the table, too. Then he seats her, and before seating himself, refreshes the wineglasses once again.

In a drunken stupor, I pick at my crab. What would normally frustrate me (painstaking process, minimal reward) is an engrossing culinary dissection. I recall watching the contestants at the Party on the Bay — their single-minded alacrity. Under Sue's tutelage, I work slow-

ly and semi-methodically. The taste of the crabmeat becomes almost secondary — I transfer morsels to my mouth without giving them much thought. Conscientiously, my fingers forage through the exoskeleton. It takes the better part of an hour to polish off three crabs apiece, about the same amount of time it takes to polish off the second bottle of wine.

With twin heaps of dismembered crabs between them, Sue and Budge linger at the table. In the twilight, she no longer looks so old.

I suppose I'm more used to her face. Instead of searching it for the depredations of age, my eyes elide the harsh truth. She's a woman, no more or less attractive than any other. She's a woman, prone to the typical thought processes of her sex. She's a woman — and we get along famously. She can't help the way she looks and acts any more than I can help the way I look and act. Which just goes to show that appearance doesn't matter at all. Didn't Plato say that?

Anyway, I'm making a quantum leap here: I'm seeing her as a definite possibility.

Thus Budge describes his wine-induced assessment. Can he be serious? Apparently he is.

Around ten o'clock — tipsy, sated, talked out, and firmer friends than ever before — we finally get up from the table. I've rolled up the fragrant offal of newspapers to deposit in the trash. Sue is not the type to worry about cleaning up a mess, but she appreciates my help. Slowly and deliberately — so as to avoid a fall — she accompanies me as far as the porch steps.

Along Beach Road, it's a crisp night and the stars are out. The tide is rhythmically hissing upon the rip-rap, and at a distance inland, an owl is hooting. Budge is aware of crab odor lingering on his fingers and chin. In the motion-sensor floodlight that just now casts its beam, Sue's face is framed in a white aureole like a dandelion gone to seed.

Standing a step below, Budge draws her to him in a friendly embrace of enough duration so that he can feel her frail ribcage and drooping breasts, and since their faces are on the same level, he kisses her tenderly on the mouth. Sue does the opposite of recoil, so he kisses her once more.

"Ooh, that's nice," she says, "but we better stop."

"Why?" I ask. "Why can't we keep on doing this? Heck, Sue, why don't we just cut through the red tape and become lovers?"

"Oh, you're a silly man. But I like you."

"Well, I like you, too. Are we on the same wavelength or what?"

"We certainly appear to be," she laughs. "But let's not take things too fast."

I kiss her two or three more times and walk home, my head confused and reeling. God, what am I doing? What am I getting into?

Again, Budge has to be pardoned for veering into the realm of fiction. No such *whys* are ever asked, nor do the follow-up kisses take place. When Sue says "stop," he stops. He sees the impossibility right away.

"Now you walk straight back to your place," she says. "And be careful."

"Sure t'ing," he replies. "Thanksh for the 'lightful evenin'"

Chapter 11

What's the best way to end this work of fiction? In the past few days, I've been looking over what I've written thus far, and it's not bad — if I may say so myself — but I need to deliver a punch line, as it were, wrap up the story with a grand finale. Not an exploding cigar, but something to warm the cockles of the reader's heart — and make her or him go hog wild with literary satisfaction.

Perhaps my protagonist could get cancer of the prostate, and in the course of his treatment at Rock Hall's free clinic, meet a nurse who is impressed by the size of his member.

Perhaps he could join a singles' sailing club and meet a pert sailorette who's going through similar personal trials — a divorcée with enough independent wealth to float his boat as well as her own.

Perhaps he could just languish at the cottage, becoming one of those colorful local characters (bearded, baseball capped) who ride bicycles with full trash bags on the handlebars. Surely, there's room for one more such person in Rock Hall.

On the other hand, he could clean up his act, i.e., straighten up & fly right, i.e., forswear his literary ambition entirely, and apply for a managerial position at one of the local marinas.

Or he could just say the hell with it and try living on a boat — a decrepit stinkpot he could pick up for a few hundred dollars, and eke a living as best he could — fishing, crabbing, selling bait — and when he felt there was no point in continuing, he could sail the leaky old tub down the Chesapeake and out to the open sea, and hope that the Coast Guard wouldn't pick him up until after he was a goner.

Thus Budge considers the options for the final chapter of his work-in-progress. In contrast to these hypothetical solutions, his own life holds no such drama. One day pretty much follows the next; he eats well, sleeps well, and gets plenty of writing done.

To be single and thrifty is the key. I've grown to love tunafish, can after can of it, and I love sardines, too. I eat plenty of fruits and veggies, grow sprouts on a plate beneath the kitchen window, make soups from stock, steam lots of brown rice, incubate my own yogurt. I want to learn how to bake bread, and I'm also thinking about keeping bees and making my own cheese and tofu.

Under the circumstances, I maintain as well-balanced a diet as any, considering how little money I spend. Here's my secret: I limit my grocery shopping to one day a week, and I don't buy much.

Indeed, he is in the parking lot of Bayside Foods, carrying a meager bag of groceries to his car, when a woman in a champagne-colored Mercedes pulls into the adjacent parking space. Swinging open her door, she views the old Corolla with what appears to be recognition.

"I used to have one just like it," she addresses him matter-of-factly. "Same color, same vintage."

She is a well-dressed gray-haired matron with well-delineated breasts and expensive sunglasses that she pushes high on her head to reveal coolly appraising eyes. Budge pegs her as a country club type — a red-meat Republican with whom he has very little in common.

"No kidding," he says disinterestedly.

Collecting her handbag and sheaf of coupons, the woman locks the Mercedes keylessly. Between the vehicles she pauses, regarding — or pretending to regard — his car with discernment.

"Why, I can't get over it! It looks exactly like my Corolla. You know, I believe it *is* the very same one."

She speaks with a New Jersey accent — flat-voweled, unmusical. Budge doesn't quite know what to make of her vocalized train of thought, but he figures he may as well play along. Lifting the hatchback to stow his groceries, he says, "Take a look in here. Do you recognize the interior? As you see, it's kind of stained up."

"Yes, yes! That big ugly spot in the middle of the carpet — oh, I remember it vividly! That's where Harold — my husband — put some paint cans to take to the recycling center, and one of them tipped and burst open. Oh, what a mess!"

She sighs at the memory. "It was a great car. Does it still run well?"

"Like a top," he volunteers. Something emboldens him to take a step farther. "By the way, my name is Budge Moss."

In the space of a few seconds she looks him up and down before concluding that he is harmless.

"Pleased to meet you, Bud. I'm Matty Klein. You know, I miss that old car. It never gave me a minute of trouble. This one," she says, indicating the Mercedes, "has had one thing go wrong after another."

"I'll sell mine back to you," he offers with a grin. "How about an even trade?"

Matty Klein's laughter is loud and prolonged.

"Oh, no thank you!" she finally says. "You better keep yours for yourself."

More seriously, she adds, "Besides, my husband only got to drive this car for a little while. I'm sure he wouldn't have wanted me to part with it so soon."

She gives me an avenue to pursue right there. The convulsive laughter, the appraising eye, the not-so-cryptic message about her husband being dead. Isn't she indicating that she's lonely? I must be indicating the same thing (shopping solo, scruffily attired, only one bag of groceries).

We chat for a good five minutes. She tells a Corolla-related anecdote and I chime in with one of my own. The way she interacts with me is unaffected and natural. Outwardly, she personifies an upper socio-economic bracket, but inwardly, something radically plebeian shines through. She's got a down-to-earth attitude, a zest for life. How I wish I could know for certain that I'm conveying the same impression!

Budge can't quite muster the forwardness to say he would like to see her again, much less ask for her telephone number. Mainly, he struggles to keep a lid on his mind's tendency to fast-forward. He is doing his damnedest to act — and think! — as nonchalantly as possible. Can he have learned something from his runaway fantasies and past errors in judgement? It seems unlikely, but it just might be the case.

I decide it's best to leave it to fate. She's arriving, I'm leaving — if we're destined to meet again, we will. I'll keep an eye out for her; Rock Hall is a small place. At least I know where she shops and the car she drives, so that's a start.

Back at the cottage, he hastens to commit his latest thought revisions onscreen.

I regard this juncture as a test: if I don't pass with flying colors, I'll fall into the same old pattern of hope and disappointment. I'll reform myself by practicing a little Zen philosophy and switching off my ever-questing brain. I won't let wishful thinking take the upper hand. I'll be down to earth with my expectations; if it happens, it happens, and if it doesn't, well — as they say — shit happens too.

Budge's newfound objectivity renders him calm, so calm, in fact, that he almost stops thinking about the woman in the champagne Mercedes. He is busy with his writing, particularly the grand denouement that will be guaranteed to knock the socks off readers who may be wondering why they haven't seen a new book from him in years.

I'm gonna make a comeback, goddammit! I'm gonna wrap up my story with a clincher that'll be the talk of the town. Here's what I plan to do: my protagonist finds a woman almost exactly his age, possibly a year or two older, and they have such great sex together that he realizes what he's been missing all along. Because of this, he subjects himself to a massive reality check as he relearns the essential give and take of a healthy consensual relationship.

He realizes that for years he's been too controlling — this is why his wife left him — and now the tables are turned. He's the one who's being controlled! The new woman in his life has a lot to teach him on the subject of respect. Sexually, she maintains the upper hand by only allowing him to do what pleases her. Her pleasure, in fact, is tantamount to anything he may be feeling, or wish to feel. She's using him — yes, flat out using him — and he enjoys it! Since when has he actually been worn out by lovemaking? Since never! Does he like it? Does the bear defecate in the woods?!

He slips into this role of awkward acolyte with a passion. For once, he's no longer calling the shots. He gives and gives and gives. It helps him relax, makes him experience every sensation with soul-piercing intensity. She tells him what to do, and he does it. He's freed of sexual responsibility; he doesn't have to worry about anything — no mind trips, no comparisons, no romanticizing, no third person point of view. The only thing required of him is to lie down with her (in bed or on the floor, or out in the walled rose garden) and be a man. Moreover, he doesn't have to do much to stimulate her to orgasm; she comes twice before he's even on the home stretch.

Yes, I think I can work the sex angle to great advantage. The more she demands of him, the crazier in love he gets. A fine fettle of a finale for such an achingly lonely and lovelorn protagonist (as I've delineated him all along). He's done with the famine, now he's getting the feast. He's practically drowning in sexual surfeit. Comeuppance, resolution, validation — these overarching themes will be rolled into one. Maybe one huge fuck scene right at the end to show he's still got the physical stamina — a subtle reminder for middle-aged male readers to stay fit. Growing soft simply isn't allowed!

During the weeks Budge is drafting the juicy conclusion of his story, he has the good fortune to meet Matty Klein again. She is at the same Mainstay concert he is attending — a rollicking, foot-stomping Saturday night featuring a boogie-woogie piano player from Detroit. Because the house is packed, he doesn't spot her until intermission, far across the room. She appears to be in the company of four women, who, by the looks of them, are her age, though not nearly as attractive.

But what constitutes attractiveness? They all have short gray hair (the heavyset lady's coiffure is bluer than the others') and they're all dressed similarly (pressed jeans, turtleneck or sweater, expensive-looking costume jewelry). They all have that time-on-their-hands look: enjoying the fruits of retirement, living on a generous fixed income. (I extrapolate that they can be doting grandmothers when necessary, but most of the time they're independent self-improvers taking continuing education and exercise classes and zeroing in on cultural events.) I'd hazard a guess, too, that they all play golf.

And yet Matty stands out. She's no paragon of curvaceousness (like the others, she keeps a stalwart posture signifying that her spine is not succumbing to Time, although Gravity continues to take its toll). Still, there's a sauciness about her features — the very quality I first observed in the parking lot. I want to believe it's more than just a facelift. It announces to the world that she's a woman of passion and a force to be reckoned with. My gut instinct urges me to get to know her better. In a nutshell, she's sexy.

"Matty! Over here! Remember me?"

She doesn't hear him, nor does she see him. He has to get closer. Coming up beside her, he touches her shoulder. Within her arc of companions, she rotates to face him with a brittle who-are-you? smile. A whiff of sororal jealousy becomes palpable.

"Matty, it's me. Budge Moss."
She looks both pleased and puzzled.

Damn, woman, don't you remember me? I'm the man who bookmarked you when we met outside Bayside Foods a few weeks ago. I'm a person who could worship you body and soul, who could reciprocate the love only you have to give, who could dedicate his priapic energy to ending your nights of loneliness. Come, let me borrow you from this gaggle of envious companions. We have a good fifteen minutes before the boogie-woogie man cranks up set two. Come away with me to the parking lot where we can talk in private.

"Do I know you?" she asks. "You look vaguely familiar."

Budge can no longer control his exasperation. "Of course you know me! I'm the guy who drives your old car."

"Oh, the nice man who bought the Corolla. Why yes, I remember you. It's good to see you again, Bud!"

"Budge. Rhymes with fudge."

Astutely, he didn't say *drudge*.

"Of course, I'm sorry. Budge."

"That's some high-powered piano playing. Is he great or what?"

Budge's comment and query are directed to everyone. Nodding presbyopicly, the ladies concur. To take up slack, Matty makes pro forma introductions, but a nearby boor's earsplitting bark of laughter drowns out her words. Budge thinks she says Lena, Loretta, Louisa, and Lorna — all of them falling short of their nominative promise — but he could be mistaken. All are, however, having a wonderful time. The small talk continues for a minute or two, and then suddenly he and Matty are quite alone.

Oh, the wonders of the vibe level! Such a beautifully choreographed scattering — I only wish it could have been captured on video. Thanks to some unspoken feminine rule, Matty has first dibs on me. The others vamoose just long enough for us to turn our casual acquaintance into something more substantial. This is what we do: she helps me memorize her telephone number. By this simple cognitive exercise, we agree to meet again — and this time not by chance.

Three days later, a Wednesday, Budge and Matty are on their first official date. They've agreed to meet at The Baywolf, a local eatery featuring an unlimited oyster menu every Wednesday evening during months with the letter R. Throughout the bustling dining room, platefuls of the bivalves (raw, fried, Casino, Rockefeller, and Rock Haller) are being distributed and consumed with dispatch, and pitchers of draft beer, too. Amid the brouhaha, Budge feels calmer and happier than he has felt in months. Across the table, Matty is explaining how she and her late husband came to Maryland's eastern shore — a generic retirement tinged with melancholy because he got progressively sicker in a relatively short time.

Yes, it's a sad story, but her telling it makes me inordinately joyful. Something's definitely happening between us, and we're not forcing it. She's as interested in me as I am in her. We seem willing to meet each other halfway.

Budge feels so *normal* to be sitting with a woman over dinner. Consuming oysters as if he hasn't eaten in days ("I'll have one more plate of everything, please."), he studies her face as she talks. He has concluded that she bears a resemblance to the late Eppie Lederer, a.k.a., Ann Landers. Fluidly, she'll alternate between solemnity and laughter. In a series of rhetorical questions, her wisdom shines through ("Well, what was I supposed to do?" "What do you think that was all about?") before she supplies her own answers. Plus, she's got compassion — a lot more than his wife ever had, by the sound of it — and she's not afraid to show it.

Knowing her only slightly — and not even that, subjectively speaking — I'm in no position to generalize, but I'll do so anyway. She's a rare find. I could do a lot worse. She's her own creation, fully formed, and she speaks exactly what's on her mind.

Across the table, I'm thinking how badly I need to update my appreciation of womanhood. Since my youth, the ground rules have been rewritten not once but several times, and I can't say I've always kept up with the changes. A man of my years, so inculcated with sexual stereotypes, has to get beyond the supermodel/playmate/puffed-up-lips-and-tits motif that society has crammed down my gulping male throat. I need to give up false images of advertising molls and Hollywood cutout dolls and indefatigable moms and queens of television shows. I need to stop kowtowing to tight skirts and cleavage and the wet look. I need to curb my fascination with the lesbian lifestyle. Furthermore, I need to stop regarding women, once captured in — or committed to — a long-term relationship (with me), as potentially sniping, nagging, browbeating harridans — the kind "you can't live with and can't live without." In short, I need to grow up.

Strong words, coming from a man who so recently

used binoculars to study the fairer sex.

"So, tell me more about yourself," Matty is urging. "What brought you to Rock Hall?"

How do I answer? Do I go into the whole divorce business and risk sounding like a loser? Do I play it philosophically and say I'm down here taking one day at a time? Better choose my words carefully — tell just enough to flesh out credibility, but retain some manly mystery. No reason to bare my soul at this point.

"My cat and I arrived here by boat. Sold the boat, kept the cat. I came here to figure out what I'll be doing with the rest of my life. Meanwhile, I'm writing a book. That's my job. I write."

Not bad! A little trite with the "rest of my life" bit, but heartfelt. Usually, just mentioning that I'm a writer melts a woman's initial reserve. Women go deeper into books than men, I'm told, hence they're always an appreciative constituency.

"That's wonderful! I'm so impressed."

"Well, I'm glad that I impress you, because you certainly impress me."

"What for?" she counters with a quizzical smile. "You hardly know me."

"I know enough about you to like you. And I like you enough to want to spend a lot more time with you."

Whew! That was a close call! I almost said, "I like you enough to want to go to bed with you." If those words had tumbled out accidentally, I would have blown it for sure. Restraining myself thus, I'm winging it as never before.

Nevertheless, I back up my statement with a steady gaze into her eyes. Putting down my fork, I reach across the table to take her hands; simultaneously sensing my intention, she offers them to me. Her fingers are warm and strong and smooth with wear. A caregiver's hands, worldly in their pressure, honest and yearning — just like my own.

"And I'm also thinking," he adds for good measure, "that I like you enough to want to go to bed with you."

Why hold back? May as well lay all my cards on the table. Too late to stay poker-faced.
"Well, that's coming right to the point, Budge!"
"If I offend you, Matty, I'm sorry."
"No, there's nothing to apologize for. I'm not surprised that the thought has occurred to you."
"Really?"

A stupid expression. Really has got to be the most overused word in the English language, and, with a question mark after it, the least meaningful. Are we implying that what we hear is a lie? Do we question the speaker's veracity? Surely, there's a better interjection to fill a conversational gap. Whatever happened, for example, to a good old-fashioned hmmm?

She grins collusively. Her brown eyes — smallish, deep-set in fine papery rings, brimming with that strange new compasssion — regard him pensively. Their fingers are still entwined. He can see that she wants to communicate something important.

"Well, I might as well tell you the truth," she begins after a lengthy pause. "I've been thinking the same thing."

146

"You have?"

Better than another really. *This conversation is taking a decided upswing.*

"Yes, I have. Don't look so surprised. I even called my doctor to ask for some advice. You see, I." Matty pauses not for effect, but because of the frankness of the subject matter. "I haven't had sexual relations for a very long time."

"Neither have I," Budge interjects. "It's been almost five months. Five incredibly long wasted months, and it's driving me crazy."

I wouldn't have confessed this to just anybody. Personally, I regard it as a stain, a black mark on my masculine character. I've been horny but I've been lazy about it. I haven't been man enough to shag, however temporarily. Even the masturbating ceased weeks ago. All my progenital equipment, mothballed. What a waste of pleasure. I might as well have volunteered for astronaut duty on the space station.

"I've gone five *years* without sex," Matty is saying. "When a woman abstains from lovemaking that long, her body stops producing certain hormones."

Her revelation, with its clinical addendum, astounds him. "Whew! That *is* a long time!" Budge is at a loss for a more cogent remark.

"Yes it is," she says. "During my husband's last years, he was too sick to do anything, although we tried various remedies..."

Five years, did she say? That's like going through col-

lege and a year of graduate school. Two presidential elections and more. How on earth did she stand it? A weaker person — like me — might have gone bonkers. It's a well-known fact that women have different coping mechanisms than men; they go out with female friends, they watch soap operas and read magazines like Women's Day *and* Good Housekeeping. *They do yoga, they garden, they write poetry, they take gourmet cooking classes. All in all, I suppose she put the wasted time to good use.*

"That must have been incredibly hard for you, Matty."
She looks at Budge and says nothing. One thing he's learning about her: she's not a complainer.
"What I try to do," she finally says, "is have a good belly laugh at least once a day."

One evening a week later, I'm at her house for the first time — a baronial-colonial mini-mansion in a gated community north of town. She greets me at the door with a kiss full on the mouth — quite an advancement from the post-restaurant buss. She's wearing a lacy black jumpsuit, her hair and makeup are glossed to perfection, and her manner is invitingly warm. It's obvious that she has expended no small effort preparing for this occasion. I succumb as any sex-starved male would: I fall instantly under her spell.

She's a terrific cook — did I mention that already? She has made a shrimp and crabmeat fritata which, by its aroma alone, promises to be out of this world — served with roasted potatoes, asparagus spears, and a tossed arugula salad. I've splurged and brought a pricey bottle, a Cabernet Franc from a Maryland winery called Fiore. We dine classically as lovers-to-be, conversing on truisms we hold dear and just happen to hold in common. We both like cool jazz. We both admire William Faulkner. We both dig the looks of Jaguars, although neither of us has ever owned one. Oh, it's remarkable, this instant groove. Two like-minded individuals — you'd think we were lifelong bosom pals! In the candlelight, I'm aware that her blurry allure (I'm not wearing my glasses) radiates beyond her features. It encompasses the laden table, the dining alcove with its cathedral ceiling and hanging plants, the Ansel Adams print, the kitchen divider freighted with pans and bowls and utensils of preparation, including the corkscrew.

Just before the triple sorbet course, as the last of the wine is poured and their wineglasses clink once more, Matty and Budge are prepared to discuss what is really on their minds. Matty has asked — coquettishly, yet quite plainly — just what he expects of their relationship. It's a sassy gambit — borrowed from the pages of *Cosmopolitan?* — and Budge finesses it with inspired straightforwardness.

"I'd like us to become lovers. In the fullest sense. That's what we both need right now more than anything else."

My declarations could be phrased as questions, but somehow the tone of her query implies that she wants to be told what to do and why. With dessert, I know I'm in a race against time. This woman is waiting to be firmly taken by the hand and led to the bedroom.

In actuality, Matty is testing Budge to see if he is 1) heterosexual, 2) actively so, and 3) interested in her enough to do something about it. Plus, she has more clinical information to impart.

"Budge, I went to see my doctor the other day, and he examined me and said that my vaginal walls were somewhat atrophied from not having intercourse for so long."

Budge gulps, mustering his most serious and sympathetic mien. "Matty, I understand completely. Believe me, if things aren't going to work out, it's okay."

"Well, I told him I was interested in having sex with a certain gentleman..."

A certain gentleman! That's me! I can't believe it! She wants me!

"...and he prescribed a topical hormone cream to apply twice a day, which I've started doing. So what I'm trying to say is that we might have to take it slow for a while."

Having drained the last of his wine, Budge regards her with what he considers to be his sultriest expression — a level lip-biting gaze.

"Matty, I'm a patient man."

"Ooh, that's so sweet of you to say!" she exclaims, reaching across the table for his hands.

"But maybe," he continues, "what we could do right now — after we finish this scrumptious sorbet — is get undressed and lie down together. Just lie naked and hold each other because it has been so long. But only if you want to."

Her fingers squeeze his. "I want to very much," she says.

Her words both excite and tantalize him. He finds himself spooning the sorbet rather quickly.

Well, Plan A isn't gonna fly this evening, but Plan B is. And maybe it's good that we take it slowly — I mean, if she hasn't had sex in five years, she may not even want it any-

more. Maybe she's reached the bodhisattva level and can do without. But no, why am I thinking this? She wants it as much as I do — hard-on, down boy! — she said so. And when was the last time I held a naked woman in my arms? It seems like fifty *years ago! I can hardly remember the lolling plumpness of a woman's breasts — hard-on, I'm tellin' ya, ease off! — or the heft of a bell-shaped posterior — jeez, how'm I gonna get up from the table with this projection in my pants? — or the silken feel of a woman's inner thigh. Just to smell a woman's skin and hair would be ambrosia of the first order.*

The sorbet finished, they rise conspiratorially from the table. A lengthy kiss follows, then an all-enveloping hug that leaves Matty palpably gasping with desire (Budge has always been good at this). But she is also a stickler for cleaning up after a meal, so she breaks away to busy herself between kitchen sink and dishwasher while Budge, at her bidding, ferries all the items from the table, snuffs out the candles, and takes the empty wine bottle to the recycling bin in the garage.

I admire her efficiency, despite the delay it causes. She keeps a spic-and-span household, unlike my wife, who insisted on leaving all the dirty dishes until the next morning. One time I asked my wife why we couldn't just attend to the mess right away, and she got so angry that she almost flung a crudded-up saucepan at me. She didn't like my questioning her way of doing things. She said I was showing disrespect. She also accused me of killing the post-dinner mood in which lovemaking was a possible option. There'd be none the next day either, if she woke up bearing a grudge, which she often did. The thought of yet another stretch of argument-induced privation caused my own anger to flare.

151

"Can you blame me for wanting to get it over and done with? I'm the one that winds up doing it anyway."

"Oh, you're impossible!" she raged. "As if I don't do any of the work myself!"

"I'm not saying that, honey..." I began.

"Don't "honey" me! I've been slaving in the kitchen for over an hour, making you a nice dinner, and all you do is complain about cleaning up!"

"That's right! You make a big mess, then expect me to make it disappear — and the next day, too, when everything's dried and nasty."

"Well, if you're going to be like that, I'm not going to cook anymore. That's final! From now on, you can do all the cooking yourself."

But it was never final; whenever she cooked the evening meal, I always did the next morning's cleaning up. Until the day she walked out, that is. Who knows what arrangement she's worked out now, or with whom?

Sidetracked by this unpleasant reminiscence, Budge doesn't notice that Matty has almost finished in the kitchen. One by one, the appurtenances and appliances have been stowed and the cabinet doors closed. She wipes the countertop one last time; it would take a microscope to detect the slightest crumb.

We could have both pitched in and gotten the job done. Together, without postponement or arbitration. As a loving husband, I was willing to help her with any task; she only had to tell me what she wanted done — and maybe offer a little positive encouragement. But this was the opposite of encouragement; this was habituated put-down with sexual repercussions. Moreover, there was something that rankled about being Mr. Cleanup the morning after — not only the delay, but the gratuitous elbow grease. Oh well, no point in getting worked up over it...

"Shall we make our way to the bedroom?" Matty is asking.

"What? Oh, sure. Yeah, that would be nice." Budge is thrown from his reverie, not quite believing what is about to happen.

Concrete steps to the bedroom! Am I climbing this stairwell for real? Is the woman treading the steps ahead of me actually going to get undressed? And what's more, am I? She seems determined to follow through with the plan. Does this mean that the long dry spell is coming to an end?

The master bedroom is large, tastefully appointed and draped, with a white ceiling fan suspended at its center. Illumination is provided by two electric candles on a long teak bureau across from the bed.

"I'll just be a minute," says Matty, veering toward the master bathroom's louvered door. "You can use the bathroom down the hall, if you'd like. Just put your clothes on the back of this chair."

Nice easy-to-understand instructions. No ambiguities. She's getting undressed behind the door and will come out fully naked, crossing the carpet to whichever is her side of the bed. I sit in the chair and remove my socks and shoes. Unbuttoning my shirt, I glance around. The bed is huge — a mahogany four-poster looming in both height and breadth. The Klein connubial mattress, upon which I will trespass... I force my eyes to look elsewhere. Several sub-dued prints, tastefully framed, grace the walls, and a bevy of family photographs is propped aslant along the bureau. A telephone occupies one end table, along with a reading lamp, digital clock, sharpened pencil and notepad. There's a small desk, too, with accordian folders and a tennis trophy. I'm in the sanctum sanctorum, both bedroom and office, and the fact that I'm here, after five years of unconducted business, is indeed a high honor.

Hearing the toilet flush, I hastily remove the last of my clothing. Now I stand naked, ready for I know not what, still in a partial state of disbelief but expectant beyond all experience in recent memory.

Matty opens the bathroom door and walks demurely into the room. She hasn't a stitch of clothing on.

For an older woman, she's nicely built. No, that sounds sexist. She's nicely built, period. She comes right up to me, and we embrace and kiss. The coolness and smoothness of her flesh is magical; I cup her buttocks, pulling her hips against mine, and of course, my penis practically jumps to attention, insinuating itself against the soft amplitude of her abdomen. Her breasts plump against my chest, twin fenders warmly cushioning. We aren't too steady on our feet, as if our brains, momentarily distracted by this crescendo of sensation, provide minimal motor control and balance. Tripping over each other, we stumble toward the bed. Matty exhibits enough presence of mind to reach out and tug down the counterpane.

"Which side do you prefer?" Budge asks, but he doesn't have to because they recline as one, comfortably and easily. Clearly, she is as hungry for lovemaking as he is, if not hungrier.

"This is fine," she murmurs. Her kisses grow more aggressive.

I endeavor to match her intensity. Really, for a woman of her age, she's hot. Hotter than I would have imagined — I mean, she's practically devouring me. But I can give as well as I get; I'm no wimp when it comes to tough love. At first we grapple more than embrace — a hyper-passionate exploration fueled by starvation and neglect. The chaste years have left her like this, and the same goes for me, albeit in a shorter time frame. Hungrily, we burn hundreds upon hundreds of calories in this bonfire of precoital gluttony.

Fifteen minutes, twenty minutes of this, and I realize that my vitality is peaking. While my ardor is undiminished — now I'm lightly fingering her and she's not stopping me — I'm expending greater physical effort. Foreplay of this duration is indeed a chore! As my energy saps, my erection, though still serviceable, becomes somewhat malleable in her grasp. This flaccidity, however, is of no concern to me, for we've achieved what we set out to do. Naked and thrashing on the bed, we've broken ground for a promising sexual future. Our fiery embrace can now subside in gentler caresses of lovingkindness as we relax side by side, quietly stroking and smooching.

But Matty ups the ante. "Let's go ahead with it," she whispers.

"I don't want to hurt you," Budge says.

"You won't."

"Are you sure?"

"Yes."

"Don't we need protection?" he asks.

Matty smirks, landing a kiss squarely on the tip of his nose. "A couple of old marrieds, celibate and randier than hell?" I'm not worried. Are you?"

"No."

"Well, what's stopping us?"

Under any other circumstance, in real life or fantasy, Budge wouldn't be so hesitant, but he still feels obliged to abide by the original ground rules – he has internalized them, it seems. Now that she has changed her mind, he definitely wants to accommodate her — of course he does! — but the fact of the matter is, he's not... quite... ready.

I move to climb on top of her, and she spreads her thighs willingly. In ye olde missionary position, I'm counting on my erection to reassert itself. Always has in the past. Matty brings her free hand into play, guiding me between her waiting wet labia. Our pelvises nudge, then grind, and I'm home — oh, she's in a fever, she wants all of me and I give it to her.

Not quite. The guiding, the grinding — that part is all true, but Budge's erection fails miserably. The more he attempts to prod, the less he has to prod with, until finally his penis has become so shrunken and useless that it's a joke, more or less, and he announces it thus.

"Looks like one part of me's gone to sleep. Wish it were just a leg or an arm. Sorry about that."

Matty looks up at him with understanding eyes. "It's okay, it happens to the best of us."

He climbs off her and they lie side by side, barely touching. He knows he needs to take it easy, just relax and not get upset. Unfortunately, he is capable of only the opposite.

A naked woman. In her own bed. Wants to get laid. Hasn't been laid in five years. What happens next? I can't get it up!

Budge feels he has to explain himself to Matty. "I guess I'm out of practice," he says.

"You're not the only one."

"I know, but it's ridiculous. I really want you, I want you badly."

"You can't win 'em all, Budge."

His dejection renders him momentarily disinterested in her flesh.

What have I gotten myself into? There's a job to be done and I'm not man enough to do it. A tradesman without his tools, a soldier without his weapon. If I found her repulsive, this state of affairs would make sense, but, truth to tell, I'm turned on by her — perfervidly so. Everything about her excites me, so why am I so... unexcited?

Wallowing so deeply in self-pity, he almost doesn't hear what Matty is telling him.

"... and he kept the pills in the medicine cabinet. I could get one if you wanted to try it."

"What pills?"

"Sildenafil citrate. Also known as Viagra. My husband took one now and then before he died. He always claimed they worked pretty well, but of course that was some time ago."

I know. Five years. Matty, you are so resourceful. "Now and then" — ha! You don't have to tell me more. You deserved a good sex life with him, now you deserve one with me. Sure, I'll try one. Why not? It won't kill me.

The pill, the glass of water, the exaggerated gulp (he was never a good pill swallower), and they lie down together again.

157

"Give it about twenty minutes or so," she says.
"No problem. C'mere and kiss me."

Resuming where we left off, I take her in my arms again. We're cozier now, not in so big a rush. There's time to dawdle over details, like fractionated kisses to overlooked places. I kiss the crooks of her elbows, for example; she kisses my wrists and forearms. Neither of us speaks — for once, verbal communication is firmly belted into the back-seat. My rational mind is shut down, too (thinking can be hazardous in the bedroom). The light is low enough to create the illusion that she's an icon or exemplar of femininity. Just the way she's breathing tells me I'm doing something right for a change. She wants me, and I have the privilege of satisfying her. Isn't this what I've been searching for all these months?

Powerfully and chemically enhanced, my erection is slowly taking hold. This time it won't be defeated by performance anxiety — kudos to the chemists and trial volunteers and marketeers, the doctors and ad writers and webmasters, the consumers and word-of-mouthers and their significant others. Kudos to the dead man who unwittingly left a dose in the medicine cabinet for his replacement. Kudos to Matty for remembering.

Bursting with gratitude, Budge gives credit where credit is due. He is almost ready to be straddled by this sexual creature. For once, he doesn't have to remind himself to look forward, not backward, to the present.